Race to Refuge

Liz Craig

Race to Refuge

Formatting: Wild Seas Formatting

Chapter One

Mallory

I was late for work and it felt like everything that could go wrong was going wrong. The session had already started and I was still trying to make it through security. I work as an aide for a North Carolina state senator. Mostly, it's a glorified gofer job when they're in session. The security guard was being really diligent with my handbag, for some reason. Usually, I'd look at it as a great way to stay safe, but today, late for work, hair damp because of a shorted-out hairdryer, clothes wet from rain, emotionally drained from the toxic relationship I was in, I was just ready to get on with it and start my workday.

Finally, I was allowed farther into the legislative building and I jogged up the red-carpeted stairs. Scott, a work friend of mine, sidled up to me and murmured, "It's feeling like a Monday." He rolled his eyes and straightened his blue and white striped bowtie.

"For a Tuesday, that's never good," I said. "But you're right. Today's got the Monday vibe going. What's happening here?"

Scott raised his eyebrows and leaned closer. "Take a look over there," he said, gesturing to a desk across the chamber.

I squinted across to a desk near the front of the

room. The Sergeant-at-Arms crouched over a rotund figure on the floor. An aide hovered anxiously nearby, talking on his phone while waving his hands around rapidly. The figure on the floor convulsed violently as if in the throes of a grand-mal seizure. More security ran in to assist.

"Is that Representative Murdock?" I whispered. "What's happening to him?"

Scott shook his head and was quiet for a few seconds before saying, "He had some sort of weird encounter before he came into the building. I was heading through security while he was and he was really shaken up about it. Said some strange man came up to him in the street and ... attacked him."

I pushed a strand of wet black hair behind my ear. "Attacked him? You mean, started yelling at him? Someone who didn't like his policies or something?"

"No," said Scott, lowering his voice to the point where I had to lean in closer to hear him. "No, I mean that he *attacked* him. Physically. The guy bit him on the neck and Murdock had to beat him off with his briefcase. Said he snarled like an animal." Scott's face, usually so laid-back was uncertain.

I spoke slower than usual, trying to process what he was telling me. "So, did the police get him?"

Scott gave a cough that was supposed to sound scoffing but sounded sort of strangled instead. "Cops? No. They wouldn't have been able to get him because he immediately lumbered off into the crowd and left. Snarling as he went."

I shivered. "Sounds like someone who is disturbed, maybe? Do you think the Representative was especially targeted?" I'd hoped today was going to be one of those workdays where I coasted at the office on autopilot while working through my personal problems. But it sounded like I needed to be right on top of whatever was going on here.

Scott shrugged. "Who knows with those types of people? But I can't imagine that was the reason. This wasn't a protester. This was someone behaving like a rabid animal." He paused and narrowed his eyes. "You haven't had a run-in with that person, have you?"

I forced a light laugh. "Of course not. Why?"

"Well, because you've got a big bruise right over your eye. Actually, I'd call that a *black* eye." He leaned in closer. "Somebody hit you, Mallory?"

"No, I just tripped last night when I was on my way to bed. Hit my head on the bed knob," I said. "Clumsy."

Scott nodded slowly again. I could tell he didn't believe a word of it. Which was perceptive of him. The truth was that it had been a rough couple of days. And I *wasn't* a clumsy person.

The rest of the morning was almost a blur. I was doing my job, but only with half my mind on what I was doing.

"Closed session," called out one of the legislators. "Everyone else can break for lunch."

Scott sidled up to me again. "What's going on?" he asked under his breath. "Closed door session? That's not on the agenda."

I nodded. "I know. Weird. But it works for me because I've got an errand to do and I've got to take a long lunch. If I'm not back in an hour and a half, can you cover for me, Scott? Tell the senator that my errand is running behind but that I'll be there soon?"

Usually Scott would be nosy about this mysterious errand. But it was obvious he was totally wrapped up in the unusual closed session.

Traffic was heavier than usual with lots of people

blowing their horns. Raleigh, North Carolina, isn't exactly a huge metropolitan area, so this wasn't what I was expecting during my lunch hour. Everybody was in a hurry. A minivan swerved past me, blowing its horn as it went and I blew back. It looked like some kid driving the car, too. I shook my head. I was starting to sound like my parents. And I was only twenty-eight.

When I got to my apartment, the parking lot looked busy with tons of cars in the parking lot.which was surprising, considering it was a workday. I picked all the polish off my nails while I waited for a parking space in front of our unit. For once, I *did* want a close spot. If I was going to just throw all my stuff in the Subaru with no boxes or anything, I wanted to be as close as I could be. At least Brendan and I lived on the ground floor. I'd never really liked being on the ground before ... too many sounds from the upstairs units. But now it was a good thing.

Finally I got a spot and backed into the parking place. I opened the trunk and all the doors on the car. Then I ran in and started grabbing everything that was mine. I knew I was going to end up leaving some stuff behind, but I really didn't care. There was no way I was going to risk a future confrontation with Brendan because I took the TV that we'd both bought. It was *his* TV now.

There are sirens everywhere as I grab clothes and toiletries and prescriptions and towels and pictures and toss them into the Subaru's trunk and backseat. Must have something to do with all the traffic and the crazy way people were driving. Maybe the cops pulled over that kid who was driving a hundred miles an hour.

The phone rang, which made me jump half a

mile. It was the land-line, too, and not many people had that number. I checked the caller ID. It was my college roommate, Annie. She was still my best friend, even though we hardly ever got to see each other anymore what with work and living in different towns.

I hesitated for a second, and then picked up. "Annie? Hey. Listen, I'm just at the apartment for a minute and I've got to get back to work."

"Have you seen the news? I mean, I know you work with government and all, but did you hear what's going on?"

Annie's voice was tight and anxious and not at all like her. She's one of the most laid-back people I know. One of those hippie-Earth-mother types who makes her own household cleaners and eats organic and that kind of thing. "No, I've had a crazy day and haven't turned it on. What's up?" An icy chill was already going up my spine, though. It was almost like I *knew*.

"No time to explain, Mallory—just—you've gotta get out of there. Out of the city. It's some crazy kind of virus or something. Like rabies. It's making infected people attack other people; then *those* people are getting sick and attacking other people."

My head was spinning so much that I sat down on the arm of the sofa that I was going to let Brendan keep. "Zombies? Annie, you realize you're talking about zombies." I gave a sort of humorless laugh. "That's sort of crazy. This isn't April Fools, is it?" But my mind went to what Scott was telling me this morning and the attack near the state house.

"Mallory, listen. Just get out. Leave Brendan behind if he's not there ... you know I think that's not a bad thing anyway. Throw your stuff in the car and get out of town. Jim and I are going to go to our getaway in the country—you know—near the border of North Carolina."

I did know. Annie and Jim lived in DC, but escaped as much as they could to their hideaway in the middle of nowhere. I'd been there exactly twice and wasn't sure I really could get myself back. Nor was I convinced that this is something I needed to do. But Annie was usually super-logical, even if she was kind of a dreamer.

Annie's voice was shrill and nothing like her. "221 Crepe Myrtle Lane. The code for the lock box on the door ... have you got a pen?"

"Yes." I poised the pen over my hand. I had a pen, just no paper.

"It's 4474. Okay? Mallory, be careful. And just go, all right? I'm serious. Leave Brendan."

I gave a humorless laugh as I glanced around the room to see if I was forgetting anything important. "I'm one step ahead of you there, Annie. Brendan and I had an epic fight this morning. You know how we've been arguing about whether we should take the next step and marry. I want kids. He doesn't. Except, this time he decided to punctuate his point with a punch."

Annie's voice was now furious. "Jerk."

I'd called him other names, actually. "It doesn't matter. It made me realize that I needed to move out. I'm just mad that I misjudged him enough to have a relationship with him for a year. What a waste."

Annie said, "Right. And now you're getting out of there and heading to Crepe Myrtle Lane. Now. Right?"

Her voice had that odd urgency again that wasn't like her. Ordinarily she'd want to bash Brendan for a while on the phone. That chill crept up my spine again. "Yes. I guess. Annie, I've got a job, you know."

"They owe you time off. Besides, they won't even

know you're gone—it's going to be crazy over there. Mallory—run. I've gotta go."

The line went dead.

Chapter Two

Ty

I was playing a zombie RPG when I heard about the attacks. A weird coincidence. Even weirder, I was playing the part of the zombie, not the zombie hunter, in the role play.

It was about time to leave for school. Most of the time, my parents didn't want me to play before school, but this morning they were distracted. It took me ten minutes to get ready for school, anyway. I scooted off real quick in the shower, pulled on jeans and a tee shirt, grabbed a granola bar and a glass of milk, and was all set. I'd even packed my backpack and made my lunch the night before, which was practically historic. But there was an online player that I knew was going to play this morning and I wanted to have a quick match with him if I could make time.

I'd signed in and was starting out with the game when a chat box popped up. Captain Crunch was the player. He usually sounded real chill whenever he chatted online. Just real laid back. I think he might have been an older dude ... maybe in college. This time he sounded urgent. *Don't go to school.*

I hesitated. It's not like I trust people online or think they're like my real life friends. I'm not stupid. They're friends. But they're different. I'm not giving out my home address or doing something idiotic like that.

But I've played with this guy a while. If I felt like I really knew anybody online, it was him. "Why not?" I typed.

There's some crazy stuff going on out there, dude. I'm in New York. I know you don't live here, but there's some kind of sick virus or something. They said on the news it's almost like rabies. People attacking other people. Seems more like zombies to me. I know it sounds nuts. But look outside. Check the news. Skip school so you're not trapped there. Don't go.

He signed out of the game and I sat there for a minute, staring at the screen. Did Mom and Dad know I was playing games? Or could I still get away with saying I felt sick?

"Mom?" I called out.

I could hear Mom and Dad talking to each other downstairs. They had that morning-stressed tone where they were flinging things around, trying to find their stuff so they could get out the door. Of course, they were usually stressed when they were around each other, anyway.

"I don't *know* where that business card is, Dan," said Mom in a reproachful voice. "It's not my job to keep up with your things."

"Mom?" I asked. "Hey, I'm not feeling so well. Could I stay home today to keep close to a bathroom?"

"Nice try, Ty," said Dad without even turning around from pouring his coffee. "I heard you up there playing games."

Mom reached out and ruffled my hair. "Sorry, hon. You've got that science test today, too, so I want you to make it."

"I've got the science nailed, Mom," I said impatiently. Actually, I had it *all* nailed and they knew it. I spent most of the time in class thinking about other stuff and still had all A's. Which made it especially frustrating that Mom and Dad wouldn't give me a break. So tactic number two, now—the truth. I hesitated for a second before saying, "Okay, the truth is that I'm worried about going to school. And worried about Ginny being at school. You're right, I was playing games. But while I was playing, I heard about some weird stuff going on. It sounded like some weird virus that makes people attack other people." There was *no* way I was going to bring up the word 'zombie.'

Dad was now doctoring his coffee with a ton of sugar. He snorted. "Ty, these games you're playing are making you break with reality. You're fifteen years old. Your brain is still developing and it's probably getting warped by this stuff you're playing. So you're saying that *zombie* attacks are happening." He finally turned around to look at me through narrowed eyes. "And what were you just playing?"

I didn't answer, just stared steadily at him.

"Zombies, right? That's what it sounded like, anyway." He rolled his eyes.

Mom, as usual, was more sympathetic. Plus the fact that she just enjoyed disagreeing with Dad. But being sympathetic didn't mean that she was on-board, either. "Hon, how did you hear about the attacks if you were playing a game?"

I sighed. It wasn't going to sound good. But I couldn't say that I saw the news on Twitter or my phone or something because my phone was still on the charger here in the kitchen. "It was a friend of mine. A guy online."

Dad was now totally ignoring me as he lifted papers still looking for the stuff he needed for his briefcase.

Mom said, "He was just pulling your leg, Ty."

"This guy doesn't do things like that," I said stubbornly. But it was pointless to argue. They were just going to say that I didn't know these online friends. Then they'd so some sort of lame safety check to make sure I wasn't giving out personal information online. "Look, have you watched the news this morning?" I pleaded.

"I certainly have," said Mom, pointedly handing me my backpack. "There was absolutely nothing on the news about any attacks when I was checking the weather."

"But that was local news. This might just be breaking on national," I said. "I don't want anything to happen to you guys, either."

"Thanks for the concern," said Dad. "But I think we're good. And I'm running late. And *you're* running late if you're going to catch the bus, Ty."

"Look, Ty," said Mom, giving me a loose hug. "You're talking about viruses, right? They can take a while to transfer and become real outbreaks. It's not like some imminent danger."

"I'm out of here," said Dad tightly. "Get it together, Ty, and get going."

"All right," I said. "Let me just run upstairs for a minute and grab something off the printer." I jogged up the stairs. I had an uneasy feeling in my stomach about the whole thing. For a minute I wondered if maybe the made-up story about being sick was coming true.

Naturally, the printer was out of paper. I set down my backpack and opened a new pack and was sticking it in the top drawer of the printer when I heard yelling outside toward the front of the house. I dropped the paper and pushed the curtains to take a look.

Then I heard my mom screaming downstairs. "Roger!"

Looking out the window, I saw one of our next door neighbors attacking my dad. He swung his briefcase at the thing as hard as he could, and he was a strong man. But this thing ... and it was a zombie ... was unaffected by the blows it was getting. It was true. And then—I did turn away and get sick.

Wiping my mouth I yelled, "Mom! Stay inside! Mom, come here!" Legs shaking I ran down the stairs, taking them a couple at a time.

It was too late. Mom had gone out to help Dad and was immediately attacked by two of the zombies. What was even more horrible ... Dad was already turning. At least, his eyes were getting a hollow, hungry look and his motions were no longer fluid, but jerky. When he turned to Mom, and I realized—and *she* realized that he wasn't going to help her—I'd seen enough.

I locked the front door and pulled chairs and small tables to block it. Then I checked the back door to make sure that it was also secure. I jerked open the pantry door. Mom must have gone to the store yesterday, because it was full of food and water bottles. I ran around the house, pulling together tote bags and boxes and throwing food and waters and a first aid kit in them, trying to ignore the sirens and screams from outside. Did I just have minutes? How strong were these things? How smart? Would they think to break a window? Would they use teamwork?

I knew I had to get my sister, Ginny. Would the zombies be at the middle school already? I needed Mom's car out of the garage. Was the garage door open, or closed? Did Dad go out through the garage or the front door? Was his car blocking Mom's? I could barely focus on what I was trying to do with all the questions flying through my head.

I forced myself to look out the front window, trying not to see my parents. And I saw that Dad's car was off to the side of the driveway. I could get Mom's car out.

I flung the stuff I'd put together into the back of Mom's van, wishing I could stop shaking and think harder and clearer about what I needed. First aid, food, water. Maybe blankets. I ran back in the house and pulled blankets and bedspreads off the guest room beds downstairs and pushed them into the van.

Weapons. Dad wasn't much help here, since he never liked guns. Instead I grabbed my baseball bat and an ax and shovel from the garage.

My camping equipment for scouts was in the garage, too, and as soon as I spotted it, I knew that was probably some of the best stuff to have. I even had water purification straws and that kind of stuff. I threw in a sleeping bag, tent, flashlights, and matches.

And all the time, zombies were scratching at the garage door and moaning.

Chapter Three

Charlie

I finished my new-employee orientation at the hospital. It was as boring as I'd figured it would be and I was ready to move on to the rest of my first day on the job. The reason I'd switched from being a salesman to being a paramedic was because I was ready for more excitement. The sales job, despite all the travel…the endless airports and planes…just wasn't providing that.

I joined my new coworker, Wes, at the ambulance parked in the hospital lot. We shook hands. He grinned at me and arched an eyebrow. "How was orientation?"

"Boring," I admitted with a laugh. "I was ready to get out of there."

Wes shook his head. "Just be aware that this job is ninety-five-percent total boredom."

I asked, "And five percent adrenaline, right?"

Wes said, "We go on tons of calls where no emergency help is required at all. We *think* we're about to get rescued from a dull shift, but then it ends up being something like a fender bender and somebody with a couple of scratches." He glanced at his watch. "We'd better get in the truck. Do you want to drive?"

I hesitated. I'd thought I'd really be more

observing today. "Do you want me to?"

"I've been driving my last couple of shifts and could use the break. Do you mind?" Wes was already heading to the passenger seat.

For about thirty minutes, I could see what Wes was talking about. Nothing was going on in this town. Apparently everyone was driving safely, using excellent fire and stove safety, and treading carefully down staircases. Wes closed his eyes and leaned his head against the window. While sitting there waiting for a call I started checking the gig for equipment and familiarizing myself with where everything was. "Wake me up if anything happens, okay?" Wes mumbled.

Then something did happen. Our computer console on the dashboard notified us of a call. "Hey Wes," I said. "I think we're about to have our five percent excitement for the day."

Wes became fully alert quickly and his eyes scanned the data terminal for more information as I started up the truck to drive to the scene. "Huh. This sounds like a weird one, too. You always remember your first call, but this one sounds like one to remember anyway. The 911 call says some man was attacked by a person who started gnawing on him. Victim is in bad shape and needs transport to the nearest hospital."

"A *person* started gnawing on them?" The siren was going and my blood was pounding. It felt good to be here, good to be on my way to help out. This was what I craved.

"That's what it says. Someone mentally disturbed I guess. The neighbors came out and chased him off and called the cops." Wes's voice was uncertain. "You know, I thought I heard something on the news on the way over here. A similar report somewhere else."

"Maybe some kind of weird gang activity? Like an initiation or something?" I asked.

Wes just shook his head. The rest of the time he only spoke to let me know when the intersection was clear on the way to the scene, just a few blocks away.

It was a quiet neighborhood—ordinarily. But today was different. It looked like all of the people who lived there were either standing out in the street watching what was unfolding, or else they were looking out of their windows and doors. Their faces were tight and scared.

We pulled up, lights still going on top of the ambulance and hopped out, running with a jump bag and stretcher to the victim who was surrounded by a group of people.

Wes, although he was a basic EMT, was giving me information about the victim in short sentences. Still breathing. Seems to be in shock. Needs tourniquet. We worked together fast to treat the victim and get him into the ambulance.

One of the neighbors wouldn't stop talking. I was so focused on our patient that I wasn't even listening. Then something she said finally sunk in. In a guttural voice, she said. "Look at him. Look at him! What's wrong with his eyes?"

"He's in shock," muttered Wes. He and I loaded the man onto the stretcher. But I looked closer at the victim's eyes. They were glazing over with a thin gray membrane. The victim was thrashing around on the board and we had to put restraints on ... with some difficulty.

"Easy there," said Wes in an even voice.

We rolled him into the back of the ambulance. Technically, since I was the paramedic, I had more training than Wes, who was an Advanced EMT. But there was no question that he had the most experience. Wes automatically climbed into the back with the patient. The patient stopped moving. Wes looked at me. "I've lost a pulse. I'll try to keep bringing him back ... just get us to the hospital."

I hopped behind the wheel, blaring the siren as I sped to the hospital. Without Wes to tell me I was clear, it was pretty terrifying going through stoplights at those huge intersections. But then I started hearing crashing sounds in the back of the ambulance and that terrified me even more. I had a dead or, at the very least, dying patient in the back. What could be making those sounds?

Should I pull over and check? Even though I needed to get this guy to the hospital before he ended up having to go to the morgue? There was a crash right behind my head and this time I spared a glance over my shoulder. I saw Wes, palms splayed on the glass partition between us. His eyes were covered with a thin, gray membrane, his mouth was slack, and he was covered with blood ... and snarling. I turned back to glance at the road, and when I turned back to look at the back window, our victim was staring hungrily back at me. Whatever soul that had made it human before was gone now.

There was no more indecision. I felt no responsibility to the creature in the back now. My mind grappled with using the word *zombie*, but it wasn't long before I accepted it, at least mentally. Although I'd like to think that I had a responsibility to Wes as a coworker, the truth was that the thing in the back was fast turning into something that wasn't Wes at all.

I decided to abandon the ambulance and drive myself back home. If I could get away from Wes and our patient before they attacked me, that is. Looking at the buttons on the driver door, there didn't seem to be a way to lock the back doors of the ambulance from the front. But I was pretty fast when running on foot. I hoped Wes and the patient weren't very fast.

I pulled the rig over to the side of the road. Clearly it would be irresponsible of me to bring these creatures back to the hospital to inflict harm on helpless patients and staff. The side of the road was a better option, despite the fact it meant I'd have to jog a long ways to my car.

Now the road was full of emergency vehicles. Police cars were screaming by, lights flashing, along with other ambulances and fire trucks. It seemed like too many rescuers for a car wreck, house fire, or other more ordinary emergency. Was this zombie threat spreading? How fast? Did I even have a shot at getting back to my house?

As soon as I stopped, I yanked the keys out of the ignition. I was thinking maybe I could lock the back of the trunk manually before Wes and the patient could get out. Then maybe I could radio in and warn people about what was in the back before they could check it out and get hurt.

But the second I stumbled out of the ambulance, so did the things from the back. They lurched toward me, mouths open.

So I hopped right back into the truck, locking the doors with a shaking hand, and took off before they could get back into the back. At least they didn't seem to have superhuman speed.

I'm not ashamed to admit that I had my siren on, too. I wanted people to get out of my way. My plan at this point was to hightail it back to the hospital, dump the ambulance there, ditch the rest of my very first day as a paramedic, get into my pickup, and get back to my house to figure out where to go from there.

Plan B was born the moment I got to the hospital and saw zombies had taken over the parking deck and were coming out of the hospital entrance. Driving over to my truck, I saw a couple of zombies standing right there. They became very animated when they spotted me through the ambulance windshield.

That was when I decided the ambulance was going home with me. And wondered if this was the worst first workday in all of employment history.

Chapter Four

Mallory

As soon as I got off the phone with Annie, I switched what I was doing. Instead of focusing on my books, I headed into the kitchen. I pulled out some garbage bags and started throwing in food from the pantry.

Unfortunately, I'd planned on going to the store today. Before ... well ... everything. So the pantry was a little bare. I did get cereal, canned foods, and peanut butter. Then I realized I needed something to open the cans with, so I threw in a can opener. And all the while the sirens were blaring in the background.

There were no water bottles in the pantry so I dumped out every container I could find and filled them with water. Then I was left with a bunch of really heavy things to be dragged out to the Subaru.

I'd just filled all the containers when I heard a bunch of yelling in the parking lot at the other end of the row of apartments. "What's going on?" I asked a woman who was standing nearby, hands clutched under her neck as she peered intently in that direction.

She shrugged a thin shoulder at me, not looking my way. "There's some woman who's flipping out. She's trying to bite people. Somebody said she was ... growling." She gave the kind of dismissive laugh that wasn't really dismissive at all—it was just baffled. "I called the cops, but no one is coming. Can you believe that? How busy could they be?"

Remembering all the sirens, I had a sinking feeling that they were a lot busier than she thought. That only strengthened my resolve to skip out of town and head for Annie's spot in the country. There sure was a lot of yelling and screaming going on, that was all that I knew.

A hand grabbed my shoulder and I jumped violently. Whipping my head around, I wasn't relieved at all to see Brendan there instead of the growling, attacking woman. Which just goes to show how I felt about Brendan.

His handsome, if rather spoiled, features were pointed into a frown. "Mallory? Why are you home in the middle of the day?" His eyes carefully avoided her bruise as if he weren't quite ready to come to terms with his behavior yet.

I didn't feel as if he deserved an answer. And now the neighbor I'd been talking to was suddenly more nosily interested in Brendan and me than the woman and the yelling and screaming at the other end of the parking lot. Her gaze traced the bruise around my eye.

"I just needed to come home briefly. I'm on my way out now, so I've got to run," I said hurriedly. I dropped my keys and he bent to quickly pick them up, holding them tightly in his hand as he rose.

He turned to the Subaru and his eyes opened wide as he saw it was packed to the ceiling with not only my stuff, but also a whole lot of food and water. "You're not leaving me, are you? Over some tiny misunderstanding?"

Now the neighbor folded her arms across her chest and leaned back against a nearby car. Settling in for the drama, I figured sourly.

"Brendan, just hand me my keys, please. I told you I need to run," I said. I noticed Brendan's hand grip my keys even more tightly—they must have been cutting into his skin.

Now he was angry. "So you sneaked over here during lunch to take all our stuff and leave? You don't have the right to do that."

"I have every right to do that," I sighed. Why didn't I see this side of him in the previous months that we'd dated? "And it's not *our* stuff. It's my stuff. Some of my things I even left there for you."

His gaze narrowed again as he studied the things in my car. "Sure looks like a bunch of *my* food and a bunch of *my* containers with water in them." He gave me a coldly calculating look. "I'm going to put this stuff back inside. We'll talk it over after you get home from work."

"No!" My voice was louder than I intended. "No. You *won't* take it back in and we *won't* talk it over tonight. There's nothing to talk over."

He didn't respond to that, instead hitting my key fob and unlocking the Subaru. He proceeded to take out a suitcase of clothes, slam the car door back, hit the lock button, and started striding toward the apartment.

"Want me to call the police again?" asked the woman, head tilted to one side. "Maybe they'll respond quicker with a domestic."

"It's not a 'domestic'," I said, the word distasteful in my mouth.

"Sure about that? That's some shiner you're sporting there," said the woman in a somewhat sarcastic tone.

I was about to respond to that, but I never had a chance. Because right at that moment, the growling woman launched herself at Brendan.

The woman I was talking to gaped at them. Then she grabbed my arm. "Look!" she croaked.

The crowd of neighbors who'd been standing around watching the confrontation was now lurching toward us. There was blood covering them and their eyes looked hollow and soulless.

Brendan was screaming now, too, and dropped my suitcase and keys on the ground in his struggle to get away from the creature—she no longer appeared human—who was attacking him.

I didn't even hesitate. I didn't try to help Brendan. I didn't call for help. Heart in my throat, I just edged up as close as I could while the thing ... the zombie, unbelievable as it seemed ... attacked him. As it was distracted, and as I was only feet away, I reached down and grabbed my keys. The suitcase couldn't be recovered since it was lodged under Brendan.

"They're coming!" shrieked the woman behind me as she ran off.

On legs that shook so hard I was terrified they'd collapse right under me, I fled for the car, locking the doors as I got in. It wasn't a moment too soon as people—creatures—who used to be my neighbors converged on my car, eyes hollow, mouths slack, and moaning.

I stuck the key in the ignition and revved up the engine. I blared the horn. And then I thought, *really*? I'm treating these things as if they were human, or someone's pet that I don't want to run over. Who cares if these things get hit by my car on the way out? Maybe that will actually help to save some innocent person from being hurt by them.

It was good that I came so quickly to this realization. At that moment, the zombies started pounding on my car, so hard that I was afraid the glass might shatter. I put the car in reverse, pushed on the accelerator, and flew backward through the crowd of once-human creatures. Some of them were on my windshield, mouths moving wordlessly, eyes gazing hungrily at me. But then I hit the road as fast as I could, jerking my steering wheel from side to side to throw them off.

I looked at my hand where I'd written the address Annie had given me on the phone. 221 Crepe Myrtle Lane. Could I get the gas I needed to travel there? What about the roads? What kind of shape were they in? Would zombies overtake me? I had no idea if I could get there. But I was certainly going to try.

Chapter Five

Ty

After I threw the camping stuff in the van along with batteries, I felt like I was seriously running on borrowed time. I searched a couple of minutes for a gas can. I did play zombie video games and I knew the kind of problems I could run into. Like no gasoline. Or nothing to *put* gasoline in when you were lucky enough to find some. I discovered a spider web covered plastic red container in a corner of the garage and picked it up. It had what was probably a splash or two of gas in it, but at least I had a gas can. I put it in the back, too.

The zombies were still scratching and moaning outside the garage door. When I realized that these zombies could possibly be my parents, I thought my legs might fall from under me. Then I got it together. My parents were gone. Even if those things *were* my parents, it wasn't the same. What I needed to do was get past them and get Ginny from the school before zombies attacked *there*.

I ran inside one more time to get my wallet. I had a feeling I didn't need it anymore, that we were heading in a direction where driver's permits and cash wouldn't get us too far. But I'd just gotten my permit. I'd only, in fact, driven by myself twice. It wasn't going to be the smoothest ride for Ginny, but it was going to serve its purpose.

I locked the door leading into the house—just in case someday I wanted to come back home. I didn't want it overrun with zombies. I got in the car. I started it up. I locked the doors. I...yes, I put my seatbelt on. Then I took a deep breath and I hit the garage door opener.

It was an instant attack. Four or five of the things, a couple of them who used to be related to me, ran at the minivan. They put their bloody faces right up to the glass, scratching the panes with their fingers. And I put the car in reverse and backed up just as fast as I could, running over one or two of them as I did.

I drove off, wondering if that was going to be the last time I saw the house I grew up in. If the last sight of it was going to be my parents, arms reaching out for me hungrily.

I put it behind me. The next step was to get to Ginny's middle school. And since there were police cars, ambulances and fire trucks whizzing by me, I figured the roads weren't going to be too easy to drive. I pushed the accelerator, forgetting how sensitive it was. I zoomed past, almost into, a woman who stared at me as if I were a zombie myself. Hadn't she ever seen a fifteen year old behind the wheel?

I fiddled with the radio to see if the news was picking up any stories about the zombies. The last thing I needed was for the middle school to go on lockdown. I could barely hear the radio over the sirens, so I turned the volume way up. "...some reports of a virus of some kind that may be spreading rapidly. It's been suggested by a law enforcement spokesman that it could be related to rabies."

Not. They only thought it was rabies because they couldn't think of anything else that might make people attack and bite other people. Anybody could see it wasn't rabies. Nobody was foaming at the mouth. And people got sick right after being infected—not like rabies, where it took a while.

I get to the middle school and pull right up to the front of the building, I fumble in the glove compartment for the notepad and pen that Mom always kept in there. I was still shaking so it took three tries for me to write: *Please release Ginny Parsons to her brother for an orthodontist appointment. Thanks, Shelia.* I hop out of the van, and run up to the school, clutching the note.

I took a deep breath, pushed my hair out of my eyes, and tried to look older. Old enough to be driving solo, old enough and responsible enough to have my sister released to my care. When you're fifteen, this isn't easy.

The office staff was already sort of looking sideways at me as I walked in. I remembered one of the women from when I was in middle school. She had short, blonde hair and wore a lot of makeup and was kind of staring at me as if she remembered me too … and didn't think it had been that long ago either, even though I was already much taller than they were, and was a beanpole. So the very tall, very skinny look wasn't helping me look older.

I cleared my throat and tried for a deeper pitch than my natural one. "Hi, I'm Ty. I'm here to pick up my sister, Ginny Parsons, for my parents. She's a seventh grader."

The blonde woman narrowed her eyes at me, thoughtfully. "Didn't your parents send in a note with Ginny this morning? Usually they send in a note and then we have the student come to the office and wait for their *parent*." She put a lot of emphasis on *parent*.

I nodded understandingly as if this were the most natural thing in the world. The whole time I'm thinking about how I probably only have minutes to get Ginny out of there—but that there's no way they're going to release her if they have *any* suspicion at all.

"Mom and Dad usually would send in a note at the beginning of the day. But they've been having sort of a rough time lately." Especially today. I took a steadying breath. "I've been trying to help them out. They did send me with this note."

I handed over the one I'd just written and the blonde woman scrutinized it, probably looking for shady grammar or misspelled words. But English was my best subject so I knew she wouldn't find them there. She pursed her lips, looking at me thoughtfully. And the whole time it felt like my heart was going to beat its way out of my chest, I tried to look as if I couldn't be less interested in taking my middle school kid sister to her orthodontist appointment.

The blonde woman exchanged glances with the other woman in the office, a woman with large red-framed glasses and a ponytail, and then back at me. "Let me make sure that you're an authorized person to pick her up. Your parents would have had to sign a form at the beginning of the year that you were authorized for us to release your sister to you."

My breath caught in my throat. Because there was no way that my parents would sign something like that. Why would they when I wasn't even driving on my own yet?

But the woman with the ponytail said to the blonde lady, "Hey, I've been in this situation myself. The nerve of the doctor's office to charge for missed visits! We should charge *them* for making us wait so long in their office. Our time is just as valuable as theirs. I'll buzz her on the intercom. What's her name again?"

I told her and she picked up a phone, punching some numbers. "Mrs. Thomas? Could you send Ginny Parsons to the office, please? She has an appointment. Thank you."

I tried to keep my face from showing the relief I felt.

The blonde woman was looking pretty sour that I'd gotten my way. "You'll need to sign your name here to authorize her being released. I don't suppose you know your sister's student ID?"

Was she kidding? I was doing well to know *my* student ID. Was this the kind of stuff Mom and Dad were expected to know? No wonder they kept forgetting everything ... there was no room left in their brains. Then I remembered the last time I saw Mom and Dad. I immediately took out my phone to look at Twitter and to forget my parents.

Twitter was full of messages about zombies. I scanned them fast to see if any of them were from people I knew or from our area. Which was when I saw something about the state house being attacked by 'people who appeared to be suffering from a strange virus.' And the state house was just a few blocks away.

Ginny cautiously entered the office, a large backpack on her back. It's not a place middle school kids really like hanging out. She had a look on her face that said that she thought she had forgotten something and maybe was in trouble. Then, when she saw me, her expression changed to total surprise.

"Ty? What's going on? What are you doing here?" she asked. She was small for her age and wasn't much into fashion. With the pink tee shirt she'd picked up at the beach last year, the denim shorts she was wearing, and her blonde hair pulled back into a braid, she could be an elementary school kid. It was just the braces that showed she must be older.

I briskly started moving her to the door. "Ginny, it's okay. We've got to get you to your orthodontist appointment."

I used a commanding voice that I was surprised I even had. But it worked because she hurried along beside me out the door. "What's going on?" she whispered to me as we quickly left.

I grabbed her arm and started running as soon as we hit the door. "Ginny, do me a favor and ditch that backpack. It's just going to take up room. Actually, even better, just dump the stuff out of it and let's keep the backpack."

"What?" she kept jogging along beside me, but now I could see she was really concerned about me. "What are you talking about? I'll get in trouble. That's all my books for school and my homework."

"Not needed anymore," I said a little breathlessly. The sirens were closer now and I squinted to see through the trees toward the direction of the state house. I couldn't see anything, but I heard what sounded like cops yelling. I bet the school was going to go on lockdown at any time.

"What?" she asked again. Now there were tears in her voice as she was seriously getting worried.

I grabbed the backpack from her, unzipped the top, and dumped everything out in about five seconds. Then I grabbed her arm again and hit the key fob to unlock the car. "Ginny, do you trust me?"

It was a rhetorical question. I knew she did. I was her big brother. What's more, we had the kind of relationship where she looked up to me. I'd never ragged on her, never done any of that stupid sibling stuff. We were good, Ginny and I.

She nodded.

"I'm going to explain everything to you. There's something bad going on. But right now, we've got to get in the car and get out of here, okay?"

As we got into the car, I could see a group of people walking toward the middle school and it felt like something big was stuck in my throat. Because they weren't people at all—they were lurching and silently munching as they walked to the school.

"Ginny, can you call the school?" I asked, pushing my phone at her. "Tell them that there's a report of some dangerous armed men heading toward the school and that lockdown is recommended."

Ginny took the phone, looking up the school's phone number. She hesitated as I sped to the exit. "But they'll think I'm pranking them. They'll know I'm a kid. They might even know who's calling. And I don't see any armed men."

"They won't believe me if I tell them the truth. It's better to give them something more believable...like armed men. Besides, it's *not* a prank, and we might save a bunch of lives." Probably not, but at least I wouldn't feel guilty about not having tried. "If you dial the number, I'll talk to them," I said. I was driving as fast as I could now.

"Shouldn't we just call the police?" asked Ginny. Her voice was thin with stress.

"They're busy." Police cars, ambulances, and fire trucks were passing us on the right and the left as we drove, sirens blaring, lights flashing. Busy, and completely overwhelmed.

She took a deep, shaky breath and dialed. Then she put the phone on speaker and wordlessly held it toward my face.

I cleared my throat, trying for that deeper voice again. As soon as the woman from the school office picked up, I said steadily, "Please put the school on lockdown. There is a group of armed men approaching the school. This is not a joke." Then I hung up.

Ginny looked at me with wide eyes. Then she gave a shaky laugh. "You sounded so grown up."

"I keep telling you that those weekly vocabulary words you get for homework are the most important thing to learn." My voice was light but I pressed harder on the accelerator. Everywhere around us I saw wrecks, emergency vehicles, and more lurching strangers.

Chapter Six

Charlie

The main problems with driving the ambulance around were that it was impossible to maneuver in heavy traffic, that these poor victims kept trying to flag me down for help, and that the thing sucked down gas like a Slurpee. I needed to ditch it. Ideally, I needed to ditch it and trade it for my motorcycle. That thing would zip through traffic like a song, use a fraction of the gas, and nobody would be trying to get me to help them.

It was killing me not to stop and help. That was the whole reason I changed jobs and became a paramedic to begin with. Right now, right here, I was in no position to help. I had no weapon. Plus, we were all quickly becoming vastly outnumbered in a short period of time. The city was no place to hang out during a zombie outbreak.

I drove up to my street. I'll admit that there are some neighbors that I'm not wild about. The guy that leaves his dog outside to bark all day while he's at work—that's very annoying. And then there's the neighbor who leaves his trash dumpster out on the street for days after the garbage man has emptied it. Just roll it back to the house, dude. It's not that big of a deal. People are lazy.

But even though I wasn't crazy about these

neighbors to begin with, I definitely liked them a lot less when they'd turned into zombies. Maybe they disliked me too, because when these neighbor-zombies spotted me in the ambulance they immediately eyed me with a gleam in their eyes with arms outstretched. Wanting to welcome me to their corrupted clan.

I had other ideas. First of all, I needed to get my dog out of there. I love Mojo like a brother—a big, furry, German shepherd brother. He trusts me and loves me and I couldn't leave him shut up in my house to starve or dehydrate. That wasn't fair to him. It also wasn't totally fair to just open the door, let him outside, and allow him to be consumed by zombies. I didn't know for sure if the zombies would attack animals, but I didn't want to take the risk with Mojo.

The only problem was that I really needed my motorcycle. Could I throw the bike in the back of the ambulance along with Mojo? The bike was a couple of hundred pounds, though, who was I kidding? Even with adrenaline pumping through my body, I wouldn't be able to lift that much weight. The only choice left as I saw it was to see if a German shepherd and a nearly two-hundred pound, forty year old man could fit on a motorcycle.

Besides Mojo, all I wanted was my bike. Sure there was a lot of other stuff in my house that I could use or would like to have, but it all mostly boiled down to my bike. Besides, if I took off on my motorcycle, I wasn't exactly going to have the space to put a bunch of things. No. The idea formulating in my head was this: get out of town first. Then *next* maybe I could scavenge around for supplies. Maybe by then, I'd even get rid of my bike and hotwire a deserted car or something.

This was all going through my head as I sat in the ambulance and watched my former neighbors stagger toward me on lurching legs. Did they have any intelligence, these things? No. Very likely not. They honestly didn't have any intelligence back when they were human, so why would that have changed now that they weren't? I put the ambulance in reverse, slowly luring the two zombies after me. They eagerly followed, clothes splattered with blood—theirs—some poor victim's?

Once we all got to the very end of my street, I quickly changed gears and punched the ambulance's accelerator as hard as I could. The ambulance shot forward and I steered it to my house at the other end of the street. I jumped out of the rig and then promptly dropped my keys in the driveway as if I were in some kind of B-movie. Glancing up, I saw the things start to stagger my way from several houses down. I took a deep breath, got myself together, ran up to the house and let myself in.

Mojo was at the door, as usual, to greet me. But this time his fur was standing up on the back of his neck. He knew something was up. And his large nose was working overtime, which made me wonder…could he smell the zombies? Did they put out a particular, distinctive smell? I reached down and gave Mojo a quick rub. His amber eyes were worried and I patted him, and then stood up quickly.

"We gotta get out of here, Mojo," I said.

Mojo continued staring steadily at me as if he understood what I was saying, or at least agreed with the intense feeling behind it. As fast as I could, I opened the coat closet and grabbed a backpack and dumped the contents out on the floor. I zipped it up and put the empty backpack on my back. I gave Mojo a whistle, but he was already ahead of me and heading to the garage door.

I've never been more grateful for a garage in my life. It gave me time to figure out how the heck to get Mojo on the bike. He'd never gone riding with me before and the bike didn't have a sidecar. I absently fastened my helmet as I thought about it...because, hey, a head injury wouldn't exactly help my situation, would it? Then I reached in my car and grabbed the garage door opener, being very careful *not* to hit the button.

Mojo would need to sit on the bike as if he were a human passenger—that is to say, he'd need to sit either behind me and put his arms on my shoulders (and this *is* a big dog, you know), or else he'd need to sit in front of me, leaning right up against the windshield, and me sitting behind him. When I realized that I didn't have any dog goggles and the wind would be bad, I figured I'd put him in front of the windshield, at least for now.

And all the while, Mojo growled softly, fur raised on his back as groaning noises and shuffling sounds came from the driveway in front of us.

I squatted down to look at Mojo. I know my urgency translated to him because he looked intently at me like he would do anything in the world that I asked him. "Mojo," I said, "come." And I stood on the other side of the bike, holding it steady as hard as I could and bracing myself. Because a German shepherd was going to try to land on a motorcycle and I didn't want to have to pick it up off the floor afterward.

And I snapped my fingers over the motorcycle's seat.

Mojo leaped carefully at the bike, landing

awkwardly on the seat and looking quizzically at me as if to say, *so, how are we going to fix this, boss?* I snapped my fingers again toward the front end of the bike and he scooted up. I got on the bike behind him, my arms around him and my hands gripping the handlebars. "It's going to be okay," I said to him. But my voice wasn't quite as strong as I wanted it to be and I wasn't sure it provided much comfort.

I started the bike in the garage with the door down, which is definitely not standard safety procedure but better than being eaten by zombies. I putt-putted over to face the garage door. "It's going to be okay," I said again to Mojo, but this time my voice was firmer and I was starting to believe it myself. I was on a *bike* that was fully gassed up. Those things were *slow*. Very scary, yes. But slow. And they were hopefully going to get the surprise of their zombie lives.

I hit the garage door button. The only bad thing about this garage door is that it goes up and down very, very slowly.

As it was going up, I heard those things snarling. And the snarling was edging closer.

Mojo snarled, too. His whole body was poised to spring, which is *not* what I wanted. I whispered soothingly to him in a soft voice.

As soon as the garage door was up enough for Mojo and me to go through without ducking, I revved the bike motor. At that same moment, the creatures shuffled into the garage, lurching toward Mojo and me with mouths agape.

I shot past them on the bike, arms tight around Mojo, murmuring to him as we went, hitting one of the zombies square on as we raced out of the garage. Sent him flying.

The neighborhood already looked infested with those things. Or, I guess I should say, my neighbors were infested. Besides the creatures that had been in my garage and driveway, there were a handful down at the end of the street. These must have been neighbors who were trying to leave for work or come in from the grocery store and were surprised by these things. Or maybe they were outside because they were trying to provide assistance to other neighbors. Either way, the infection rate, as I'd seen for myself in the ambulance, was very fast. Too fast. I didn't feel bad about not trying to take provisions with me before I left.

But I needed to get them soon. I needed to get food, water, and some clothes soon before everyone else started scavenging and everything ran out. There was a grocery store close to the edge of town. The only thing was that there wasn't a whole lot that was going to fit in the backpack I was wearing. This was the one place where a motorcycle was something of a pain——no backseats to store goods.

It made more sense for me to get tools to provide myself with the things I needed. Water purification equipment. A knife. A gun and ammunition. A collapsible shovel. Seed packets maybe. I had this terrible feeling that I needed to be thinking long-term with this. Anyway, if I was prepared for long-term problems, maybe I wouldn't need to end up using them.

Clearly, I needed to head out of town where the population wasn't as thick. Here in Charlotte, there were just too many people around. Those people had the chance to become zombies. That meant that the greater metro area could end up, worse-case-scenario, with a million zombies running around. I didn't much like those odds. I'd rather zip out to the country somewhere where I could fight off far fewer of these things.

So that's where I headed. To the store on the far edge of town to just get a few things to tide Mojo and me over for a short while. And then to the camping goods store to stock up on supplies for more of a long-term camp. I'd get out of town, and then I could really think for a while on where a good place to set up camp would be.

Sirens were still screaming by me as I zipped down the road. And now we were starting to encounter the problems that I'd envisioned when I decided to get the bike to begin with. A huge traffic jam. The ambulances were honking their horns, the police cars' sirens wailed. I saw a few families that looked like they had half their possessions in the back of their car. And they were all totally stuck in traffic.

I heard a scream behind me...somehow it rose above the cacophony of the racket. I turned to see zombies beating on the glass of a car about twenty yards back. And here Mojo and I were sitting out in the open.

This is where a bike comes in handy. Ignoring the honking horns and some rude words coming at me from open windows, I carefully maneuvered between them all, until I got to the point where I absolutely couldn't move forward anymore because of an accident that stretched across the road.

I took a deep breath, decided that the cops were all totally stuck in traffic anyway, and moved onto the sidewalk and drove there until I could get through all of the trapped cars and emergency vehicles.

As we finally really started moving, I could feel Mojo start to relax. He almost seemed to be enjoying the ride. I was glad that he didn't have the big picture of what might be facing us. He hadn't turned to see what was going on behind us, either. And maybe I needed to take a cue from him.

So that's how we made it out of there. Driving on the road, driving on the sidewalk, sometimes going off-road. Until we made it to the edge of town where there was a last-stop grocery store. It was the kind of place that was a little off the beaten path. The kind of place that was also out of touch, maybe. It didn't have a television or a radio, probably. Which was a good thing. It meant that I had half a chance of getting in there.

"Mojo, stay," I said softly.

His amber eyes pleaded with me to take him in.

"I'll be right back," I said. And then I hurried in so that I wouldn't have lied to him, crazy as that sounds.

The proprietor was anything but on high alert. He was lazily eating a sandwich. I quickly grabbed a few water bottles, some ground beef for Mojo, and some of those ready-made deli sandwiches for myself. Not much room in the backpack and I didn't need to take up all the space before I got to the sporting goods store.

I paid in credit. Because, the way things were going, nobody was going to make good on their credit card payments in the near future.

I hurried outside and stopped short at the door. Mojo's fur was up again and he was growling from the bike. He turned his head and gave me a meaningful look. I quickly glanced around. "What is it, buddy?" I murmured. I didn't see any of the creatures lurching around. But I quickly swung the backpack on my back and hopped on the bike, arms tight around the German shepherd as I started the engine. I believed

Mojo. If he thought something was out there, something was out there. I wasn't going to be stupid. The dog had a huge nose and huge ears, after all.

As we were speeding out, I saw a zombie staggering up a hill toward the store and gave Mojo a quick rub.

Chapter Seven

Mallory

I figured I should use GPS to try to get to my friend's place in the country. At least, that I should try to use GPS while I still had it. I had a terrible feeling that it wouldn't be long before we lost the internet and wireless data. There were actual people who kept electrical grids going and cell towers working through electricity. I could remember the first leg of the journey, but wasn't really sure about how to get the rest of the way there. I hoped when I finally got out of the city a little way that I could pull safely over, GPS the location, jot down the directions, and continue on my way.

The catch in that plan was the word *safely*. Because it seemed to me that, even though I hadn't spent much time at all at the apartment moving out, conditions in Raleigh were quickly getting worse. Traffic was badly backed up to my right, and glancing over I saw that there was an ambulance that had crashed into a firetruck. There were so many emergency vehicles flying down the road that it was probably unavoidable.

But when I peered closer I saw that the two vehicles appeared to have been abandoned. Abandoned? Or were the occupants chased out? I felt a shudder up my spine and kept driving as quickly as I could. Which wasn't very fast.

I was still in the city when the sirens got even louder and traffic slower. My breath caught in my throat. There were those creatures... those zombies... lunging through the streets and attacking policemen and rescue workers. The policemen were shooting them, using their weapons right out in the street, and the zombies continued pushing forward, arms outstretched and mouths agape.

Down a side street, traffic was at a standstill due to an accident or some other jam. I saw a woman dressed in business clothes abandon her car. She'd taken off her shoes and was weaving through the stopped cars and running away, two or three of those creatures following her. The only good thing seemed to be that the zombies weren't as fast as uninfected people.

I was moving slowly away when I noticed an old man with white hair and a neatly-trimmed beard who was limping as quickly as he could away from a crowd of infected people that was moving toward him. I recognized him as a homeless man that I had seen for years on my way to work and home. Every day I'd seen him and felt a twinge of guilt. I felt bad every day for not helping him, for not at least smiling and looking him in the eye. Despite his situation, he always looked strangely dignified. He always took care with his appearance, wearing threadbare but clean clothes, his white hair usually getting the best of him as it stood up in a halo effect.

I'd tell myself that I was a single woman and didn't need to get personally involved in helping him. I'd remind myself that I gave money to charitable institutions that helped the homeless. But I always still felt that twinge.

Now here he was, desperately hobbling away from these creatures, his possessions still in the small backpack he always carried. His gaze met mine— frightened, questioning. And I immediately pushed open the passenger door for him.

He stumbled in, swinging in his bad leg with some trouble. He pulled the door shut and I hit the door lock as the zombies reached the car. I pressed my foot hard on the accelerator and the car jerked forward. "Hang on," I muttered to him. Now was the time to speed. I didn't think anyone would be handing out tickets. And clearly, we needed to get the heck out of town.

"Thank you," he said quietly as he set the backpack on the floor of the front seat.

Somehow this made me feel even worse about not helping him in the past. Let's face it, I'd gotten him out of there to assuage my own guilt for passing him by, for totally ignoring him in the past.

"It's okay," I said, sounding somehow irritable. I pressed my lips shut as I sped down the road. Fifteen minutes later, I felt myself relax a little as I saw a relatively clear path out of town. We weren't going to get stuck in any traffic jams. We were going to be able to escape the city.

"Where are you headed?" asked the old man politely.

I noticed the pronoun he'd used. So he was definitely not making any assumptions that he was along for the whole trip with me. This was a good thing. I'm not sure how Annie was going to take my showing up with a homeless guy in tow. And Jim would be looking at me like I was crazy, too.

"Do you need to drop me off along the way?" he asked, his voice gently understanding. "It's okay. You don't know how much I appreciate you helping me escape."

I shocked myself by saying, "I'm trying to get to a safe place in the country. It's a house my friends own and they've invited me to come. I'll bring you along, if you like."

His clear blue eyes were grateful. And with a skill that I, as an insomniac, admired, he fell deeply asleep with a trust in me that was almost childlike.

He didn't wake up until I stopped the car to check the GPS. It felt like a safe spot. There were no surrounding homes or buildings. I had the doors locked, too. I pulled out my phone and sighed. Maybe the car charger had a short in it, because it was seriously low on battery. I opened the GPS program and carefully punched in Annie's address with one finger.

That's when he woke up and gave me a questioning look.

"I'm not exactly sure where we're headed," I explained. "I have a general idea of where to head, but I need more detailed directions." I frowned at my phone, which was moving very slowly.

"Is it pulling up?" he asked.

"Maybe. It sure is slow, though." I looked at him thoughtfully. "I'm Mallory," I said, holding out a hand. "Good to meet you."

He beamed at me, bright blue eyes pleased at going through the old formalities. He held out his own weathered hand. "I'm Joshua," he said.

"Nice to meet you," I said a little absently. At long last the directions were pulling up. "I'd better jot these down before I lose all connection."

Joshua immediately said, "If you've got paper and a pencil, read out the directions to me and I'll write them down."

I watched as he carefully wrote the detailed directions in a neat print. Then he had me read them back to him as he checked his work for errors. Satisfied, he laid the paper down in the center console. "It looks as if it will take a couple of hours to get there from here. How are we on gas?"

He was touching on one big area of concern for me right now. "We've got a little over half a tank. And this car doesn't exactly go light on gas, either. It's not a gas *guzzler*, but it definitely can use some up. When we see a station, I'm going to try to fill up," I said.

We continued on again until it was dark and getting late, Joshua dozing on and off as we went. Finally, I pulled to the side of the road. It was a very quiet road and we hadn't passed many cars along the way. And on this even smaller road, I hadn't seen any other motorists.

"I'm thinking we should stop for the night. Unless you'd like to drive, Joshua?" I asked. I still could hardly believe I was being so trusting. The old me would have been worried about allowing Joshua to take control of the car.

He smiled gently at me. "I wish I could help out with the driving, but the truth is that it's been a number of years since I've driven. Maybe in an emergency, I could help in a pinch, if we were really desperate. But now...why don't we just set up camp? You look as if you could really use the rest and you won't get good quality sleep sleeping in the car."

"Although at least in the car, I'll feel safer," I added.

He nodded. "Although I'm guessing the threat here would be very small. We don't seem to be around any cities. Finding a safe place to bed down is one area where I've had a bit of experience."

I flushed a little at not having figured that out for myself. "I guess you'd have to be an expert."

"And I'm also very good at pitching a campsite," he continued. He opened the car door and stepped outside. He seemed to be listening very hard. Then he stuck his head back inside. "I think the coast is clear."

He thoughtfully studied the things in the back of my car. Then he took the small backpack he'd brought into the car with him and took out a plastic tarp that had been carefully folded up. Using sticks and the tarp, Joshua carefully constructed a makeshift tent in no time at all.

I smiled at him, giving muted applause when he was done and he smiled at me. "You know, Joshua, that's a very useful skill to have. Unlike being a government aide. I have a feeling my skills aren't going to translate very well to this situation."

"Like my skills wouldn't translate to yours," he said, spreading his hands out.

"So, maybe I need to be thinking about more camping-related equipment," I said. "Tarps appear to be very useful."

"They could at least help you on the way to your safe house," he agreed.

I studied him again. He always spoke so deliberately. He never included himself when talking about Annie's house. Was he wondering if my friends would share my hospitality? Maybe it was something I should wonder about, too. Although I think Annie and Jim trusted me.

Joshua interrupted my thoughts. "It might also be a good idea for you to learn how to hunt. And maybe to grow a garden."

I hadn't quite wrapped my head around the fact

that this could potentially be a long-term crisis, despite the fact that I'd put most of my possessions in my car. I was still dressed in work clothes, for heaven's sake, although I'd traded out my heels for flats in the car. Squaring my black pencil skirt, crisp white blouse, and sensible jewelry with hunting and farming was hard for me to do.

Plus there was the squeamish side of me that never really liked to acknowledge where my food actually came from. It wasn't that I was a *vegetarian*. I wasn't. Except for sometimes ... sometimes I'd hear a news story about food processing or something and it would mess me up for weeks. Then I *would* be a vegetarian.

"I'm not sure if I'd make a great hunter. And I'd have to do a lot of research to figure out how to grow crops," I said. I caught myself. "I'm not sure about how I'd get that research done, either. No internet, right? And I probably can't exactly pop over to the library."

"I'll show you how to do some easy hunting," Joshua said. His voice was urgent.

I gave a sort of startled laugh. "Right now? But we have a car full of food, Joshua. I don't think I'm hungry enough to even eat whatever it is that we might kill." The word *kill* sat uncomfortably in my mouth and I hoped another vegetarian streak wasn't coming over me. "Besides, I don't even have any weapons."

Earlier today, confiding in a homeless traveling companion that I wasn't armed against would never have happened. It was funny how quickly he'd had earned my trust.

But Joshua was oddly insistent. "This type of hunting won't rely on weapons. It's a snare used to trap small animals. I think it's important for you to learn. There won't always be a car full of food. You should save that food for a more needy time where maybe there isn't food we can quickly capture."

He seemed almost distressed in his concern that I learn this technique, so I quickly said, "All right, Joshua. I'm sure you're right. Show me how it works."

His shoulders relaxed a bit and he delved into his small backpack again. He pulled out some thin wire that looked like picture hanging wire. "You could also use this," he said, pointing to a pair of headphones next to me.

I grinned at him. "I guess it's good they can be put to some use at some point. I have a feeling my iPod isn't going to stay charged forever."

Joshua smiled back as he reached again in his backpack. Next he pulled out what looked like two pieces of wood that branched out in a way that made them nest together. Apparently, one of them staked into the ground and the other to something else. I watched as he carefully scouted around the area near our car, looking for some sort of signs. Then he looked up at the various trees and foliage around us.

He motioned me to come over. I still felt a little silly in my work attire, checking out my snare trap location. Who'd have thought? I also felt remarkably unprepared. When was the last time I'd even gone camping? Middle school?

Joshua didn't treat me as though I were silly, though. In a clear voice he pointed ahead of us. "Can you see the signs that small animals have come through here?"

I peered at the ground and cleared my voice. "I can see that it's some sort of narrow trail. A well-worn animal path?"

He nodded. "Look over the hill here."

When I walked up, I saw a small stream at the

bottom of several hills. "Water source," I said.

Joshua pointed at the ground. "We haven't had rain recently, but if we had, you would be able to see tracks in the mud. Or maybe a nearby burrow. You can definitely see other signs." He pointed to a pile of small droppings. "So we know this is a good location to put up a snare trap. Knowing a good spot is half the battle."

He continued patiently showing me how to set up the basic trap, stopping from time to time to make sure I was following. And the weird thing was that I felt much safer in the exposed woods with this elderly homeless man than I'd felt at home with Brendan.

Chapter Eight

Ty

Ginny hung onto the passenger door of the minivan until her knuckles were white. I couldn't blame her—she'd never even been in the car with me driving before. And I was driving pretty fast, hoping that we could get out of town before the roads got clogged up with people trying to escape.

The main road out was already jammed with cars. Some were emergency vehicles, some looked full of people. There were a lot of horns honking.

Ginny said in her quiet voice, "We could go that back way. Do you know the way? It's how Mom takes me to skating practice when it's rush hour."

I'd been back there a couple of times, but didn't really know the way. "Can you give me some directions?"

I heard Ginny draw in a deep breath and sit forward in her seat. I could tell she was funneling as much focus as she could into where she was. "Turn off at this light."

Not that I stopped at the red light.

Soon we were on a curving, narrow back road with a lot less traffic. But I was still driving as fast as I could, right up to the time where we finally got to the edge of town. When we drove into the rural area north of town, I finally felt myself start to relax.

"Ty, where are we going?" asked Ginny softly.

"That's something I've got to figure out," I said. I tried to sound strong and confident as I said it, which was tough since my head was pounding and I felt totally lost. All I'd known was that I had to get Ginny and that we had to get out of the town. After that point, I really hadn't put a plan together. "I'm going to drive a little farther out and then we're going to sit in this locked car and I'm going to map out where we're heading and what the short-term plan is." It was to survive, but I sure wasn't going to tell Ginny that.

We continued for a few more minutes and I could tell that Ginny had a million questions on her mind. Finally she asked in a hesitant voice, "Why is there so much stuff in the back of the car?"

I glanced over at her tight, pale face. "Ginny, something terrible is happening. Some kind of virus is making people sick and then those people are trying to hurt other people. The town is going to get taken over by those sick people, and if we stayed, we wouldn't be able to survive. I threw a bunch of stuff in the car that I thought might help us if we were out in the country for a while." Until I could figure out how to get us more food and water.

She took this in and then glanced back in the back of the van again. "So ... food, camping equipment, water."

"That's right." I was glad Ginny was taking this as well as she was.

"Toilet paper?" she asked in a worried voice.

I shook my head. "I was in a hurry."

"Clothes?" Her voice was even more anxious.

Obviously, Ginny would have focused on different things.

"Ginny, I just didn't have time. I wanted to throw

stuff in the van and then pick you up from school."

She was quiet again for a few minutes and there was a quiver in her voice this time. "My retainer? Did you remember my retainer?"

At first I felt this tired anger bubbling up. Then I took a deep breath. She was scared. She didn't understand. She thought things were going to be the same. Or she hoped they were.

This time, instead of sounding strong and confident, I went with gentle. "Ginny, it doesn't matter. Your retainer. It's going to be okay."

"But Mom is going to be so mad," she said, eyes moist.

"Ginny, Mom didn't make it." My voice broke a little on the words, even though my voice had finished changing a while back.

"Dad?" she whispered.

I shook my head again. And this time I felt a prickle of tears behind my eyes, too.

"So it's just you and me?" she asked quietly.

I nodded. "But Ginny, I'm going to do a good job taking care of you. I promise."

"You've done a good job so far," she whispered, her voice breaking a little. "You got me out of there. There were sick people heading to the school, weren't there?"

"And we called to warn them," I pointed out. But she knew and I knew that those kids and teachers could only stay in the school for so long before food ran out. The cafeteria didn't exactly plan for an Armageddon when it ordered supplies.

I fished around in the center console until I found the iPod that Ginny had left in Mom's car. "Here. It's a lot to take in, right? Just listen to music for a few minutes while I sit here and think about what our next move is, okay?"

Ginny looked sad. "It's going to run out of battery. And I didn't have a charger in Mom's car."

"Enjoy it while you can. This has been a bad day, right? This is a good day to listen to it."

She fished out her headphones from the backseat somewhere and reclined the passenger seat a little. She looked out the window while I took out a pen and some sticky notes from Mom's glove box to figure things out.

Mom had gassed up the car recently, so that was good. But we were going to need gas, and sooner than later. The van wasn't the perfect car to take because it did use up a lot of gasoline. But I didn't exactly have a choice at the time. I wrote *gas* on the paper.

The food and water wasn't going to last too long, either. I added them to the list. Although the water purification sticks were really going to help long-term. I could use some more of those. I put Ginny's toilet paper on the list although that was a little more of a luxury item, considering. A better weapon than the ax, shovel, and baseball bat would be good, too.

But if I went to a big store like Walmart, would they know about what was going on in our town? How far had the news spread? I didn't have money with me … not enough, anyway. If I just walked out with the stuff then security would probably stop me. And if the Walmart had already been deserted by panicking people, then there might be zombies around. Everybody knew you weren't supposed to go to malls or places like Walmart in a zombie outbreak. At least on my game that was something you didn't want to do.

I remembered that there was a sort of country

store that was out a ways that Dad and I usually stopped by on our way out to go fishing or camping or whatever. Dad knew the guy who ran it because he'd been there for years. Maybe he could do us a favor and give us some supplies. If I explained what was going on and didn't sound crazy while I was doing it. Wouldn't he think my sister and I were running away? I decided it was my best bet, though. That was in a quiet enough place that if there *were* zombies there, there wouldn't be too many of them running around. I'd been there enough, too, that I knew where it was. Sort of.

After that, though, where was I headed? I took responsibility for Ginny, but it would be great if I could hand that over to an adult family member instead. Then I thought about Nana. She lived in senior living even farther out of town. I remembered it was a secure place, too—they didn't want their memory care residents to be able to get out so the place was really locked down. And locked down from the inside was a good thing in a zombie outbreak. I'm sure I could knock on the door and persuade somebody to let Ginny and me in—especially with Ginny being so small. They'd probably take pity on us and let us in.

They'd have probably more food on the site than the school would have and a lot less appetite for eating it. And beds to sleep in—maybe an extra room or two. It would be good to sleep hard and then make a better decision about our next move.

Ginny was looking at me with that anxious frown making a line between her eyebrows. I gave her a reassuring smile and she pulled out an earbud to listen to me. "I know what we're going to do," I said.

She relaxed a little, relieved. She didn't even look like she wanted to *hear* the plan, she just wanted to know that I had one.

I started the car up again and sped down the road until we got to the country store. It looked just the same as always. There was one gas pump outside and the stone building had one of those decorative flags outside that said *open*. There was only one vehicle there, a pickup truck that probably belonged to the owner. I couldn't remember the guy's name and hoped that he would remember me better than I could remember him. If he could just let us have some of his store stock, we'd be in a much better situation. I could even tell him that the next time Dad came through, he'd be sure to reimburse him. Then his name came to me ... Bo. It made me feel more at ease to know his name ... like we really did have a connection with each other.

I pulled the car right up to the door and hesitated, thinking things through. Maybe I should leave the car running. But was the danger really that close here? How quickly was it spreading? Would leaving the car running make me look like I'm some sort of thief?

Ginny reached for the door handle and I put out a quick hand to stop her. "Hey, Ginny, just let me look around first and make sure the area is clear, okay? Then, if I make a signal, you can come in and help me get supplies."

"You mean leave me in the car alone?" Ginny's face was uneasy.

"Just until I make sure it's safe for you to go inside," I said calmly. But inside, my heart was beating so hard that I was worried she could hear it sitting next to me.

"Don't you need to take a weapon or something in?" she asked, pointing to the bat. I guess she figured that the bat was there to defend us and that I wasn't planning on any recreational apocalyptic playing.

I was surprised. Maybe Ginny was going to adapt better than I thought. "I would, but I'm worried it's going to make me look like a thug. If I look like a thug, I don't think Bo is going to be real motivated to give us free stock." In the distance, I heard gunfire and hesitated again. We *were* out in the country. Was this just good old boys going hunting for deer? Or was it people defending themselves? "Ginny, listen to me. If I come out now and I've been attacked in some way—scratched, bitten, something like that—and I'm trying to get back into the car, you don't let me in, okay?"

Ginny's eyes were huge and her breath caught. "Ty, I don't want to be by myself. What would I do?"

"You'd drive out of here. As fast as you felt safe doing."

"I don't know how to drive!" A red flush crept up her neck and along the side of her face.

"It's easy." I spent a few moments showing her the controls and the pedals. "I'm even going to leave the car running so that you don't have to worry about starting it up."

"I can't even reach the pedals!" Ginny was definitely about to cry now, and that's the last thing I wanted. And she *was* pretty short.

"Just sit on the edge of the seat and you'll be able to reach them. Look, I'm going to pull the seat all the way up, just in case. I don't think anything is going to happen. Really." I gave her what I hoped was a confident smile as I heard more gunfire in the distance. Then I took a deep breath and got out of the car, motioning to Ginny to lock the door behind me.

Chapter Nine

Charlie

Mojo started relaxing again as soon as we got back on the highway. For me though, the highway was anything but relaxing as once again I was driving off the road half the time, trying to get around traffic jams and the wrecks causing them.

He also probably wouldn't be too happy to know what my plans were. I wanted to stop by the huge sporting goods store on the way farther out of town. This place was one of those huge warehouse-style mega-stores ... a sportsman's paradise with all the hunting, fishing, and camping equipment you could possibly imagine. I could only hope that every able-bodied man in the city hadn't gotten the same idea. I wanted to stock up on some things that could help Mojo and me in the long run: stuff like water purification, guns, things like that. Being self-sufficient was going to be important since stores would probably start getting looted and cleaned out soon. Or overrun with zombies. Besides, there was only so long that fresh foods would stay fresh.

Another thing I wanted to do was to get in touch with an old high school buddy of mine who was in the army. He was sharp as a tack but too lazy to ever really advance much in the ranks. Still, I was guessing that he could be a real font of information. Once I

LIZ CRAIG

grabbed these supplies I wanted to find a place to stash them. Getting them out of the store wouldn't be real easy as it was. I might have to make two or three trips on the motorcycle to dump things out and come back for more. But I didn't want to give up the bike yet. It hardly used any gas and could zip around almost any obstacle in its way. And no zombie was going to catch Mojo and me on that thing. So the temporary plan was that I was going to get Mojo and me settled somewhere away from the city with camping supplies, and then I'd try to put a call out to my buddy and see if he could throw a little light on the situation.

This sporting goods store was called Outbound Outfitter. And it was something to see. It was a kind of mecca for outdoorsmen. The whole design of the place was to attract attention to itself. It had the world's biggest fishing rod on one part of its roof, a fake boat on another part of its roof. It was on the top of a huge hill next to the interstate so that you couldn't miss it driving by. I can bet that any husband on his way to a family wedding, reunion, or something else was probably begging his wife to take the exit just like a kid wanting to go to Disney World. But silly as it looked, it was chock-full of guns, ammunition, and camping equipment.

At least, it *had* been. Right now it looked as if a few guys had the same brainstorm I had. There were definitely cars and trucks there, and some of them looked like they were already loaded to the gills with merchandise from the store. The only thing I was unsure about now was if we were in looting mode or legitimate purchasing mode. Then I saw a guy rushing out with his arms full of ammunition. He was wearing a forest green Outbound Outfitter golf shirt. Yep. Looting mode. Especially if we'd gotten to the point

59

where employees themselves were doing the looting.

I cut the engine and was about to tell Mojo to stay with the bike when I realized that nobody was probably going to say a word to me about a German shepherd coming into the store. So when Mojo's eyes pleaded with me to take him in, I did. When I whistled for him to come, he joyfully bounded off the bike, grinning his dog grin, and ran into the store with me.

The first thing I needed was one of those huge duffel bags that you can either carry or wear on your back. The kind the military uses ... like a 30x50. That way I could cram as much stuff into it as possible, heft it onto my back, and hopefully still be able to handle the bag and the dog on the motorcycle until we could get to a spot where I could stash everything.

There were probably half a dozen guys in there, flinging stuff in boxes. I was hoping they weren't being real organized with it so there would be something left for me. There weren't many guys, but the ones that were there looked like they were serious stockpilers. The store was huge with a hardwood floor and vaulted ceilings that were supposed to make you feel you were in some kind of lodge. It had a ton of equipment and carried equipment for fishing, hunting, boating, and camping with ATVs and even tractors thrown in to boot. Mojo trotted after me as I hurried over to where I knew backpacks and duffel bags were. The large duffel bags were still in stock, I saw with relief. When you don't have a Plan B, it's good to see that Plan A will work.

I wasn't going to randomly throw stuff in my bag like the other guys in there. I hurried over to the water purification equipment first. That's when I realized the men in the building with me were not thinking things through. That's because *all* of the stocked water purification equipment was on the shelf. There were iodine tablets, personal water filters, water bottles fitted with filters, and even some very expensive water filtration systems that looked longer-term. I quickly started sticking them in the bag.

A minute later, one of the other "customers" came to his senses. At least, that was my interpretation of the unexpected shove in the middle of my back. "I'll take one of those," he said in an ominous voice. Mojo's fur stood up on his neck again and he made a low growl that best showed off his impressive collection of extremely sharp teeth. I could see that Mojo was giving the guy second thoughts about roughing me up, although it was an indication of how desperate he was that he didn't immediately back away. Considering that he was well over six feet tall and looked like he worked out every day, I generously decided to let him grab the last one on the shelf. I moved away, hoping he wouldn't demand to look in my bag. He didn't. I guess he figured that the other men had pilfered the rest of the equipment.

Mojo and I moved through the rest of the store, picking up the most important stuff in this first go-round. After the water purification, I went for the first aid kits before I ended up at the hunting section of the store where all the firearms were stored. Unfortunately, this had been one of the first things that the men in the store had thought about … weapons. And, don't get me wrong, weapons are very important in a zombie outbreak. But you can't drink weapons, eat weapons, or bandage yourself with them.

Luckily, the other men in the store had again proved their lack of foresight. They'd decided to swipe the biggest firearms the store carried. I guess that was just their gut reaction: those creatures are scary and I need a big gun. They were going for shotguns and all I really wanted was a .22 and a box of 500 rounds of ammo. It wouldn't be too big to carry, wouldn't recoil much, and wouldn't be very loud. I suspected lots of noise might attack the zombies, and I didn't want anything that was going to make too much racket. I picked up a crossbow and stuck it on my back under the duffel bag. A sharp knife also went into my bag. No one was interested in the ski section at all, which I thought was a mistake. The ski goggles could come in handy if you were trying to avoid getting zombie bits in your eyes. I also picked up a lot of rope, a compass, a mess kit, a folding shovel, a pouch-style water container, a tent, a tarp, a poncho, emergency blankets, hand-crank flashlights, a pair of binoculars, and flint to make fires with. And duct tape. Here, the guys in the store probably just went on autopilot when they headed for the duct tape because there were only two rolls on the shelf. That's automatically what you get in almost any crisis: lots and lots of duct tape. Even if you can't immediately think of a reason for it.

The camping section had MRE type foods in pouches. I stuffed my bag with as many as I could. They were light to carry and I wouldn't have to worry about cooking them. And the meals were good for forever. I wasn't sure if they *ever* really went bad.

Finally, I headed for the fishing section of the store and got one of those really tacky looking fisherman vests with all the pockets and put it on. I figured I could use as many pockets as possible and being a fashion plate wasn't going to help me survive. I took some of the smaller things out of the duffel and stuck them in the pockets.

I whistled to Mojo and we jogged for the door. Like I said, I had every intention of returning for round two of looting the outdoors store, but as Mojo and I were trying to get out, a crowd of people forced their way in, pushing each other, eyes wide. They weren't going to be happy to discover there wasn't much stuff left on the shelves and I didn't want to be one of the people holding supplies when they figured it out.

Since the two huge front doors were jammed with people trying to force themselves in, I headed for a smaller, emergency exit on the side of the building and Mojo and I slipped right out. But now that we were in the parking lot there was another problem. Some guy was hovering over my bike, messing with the engine. Trying to hot-wire it and take it for himself.

I wasn't going to moralize. I just looted a store, right? But I wasn't going to meekly give up that bike to some middle-aged guy trying to hot-wire the thing, either. "Mojo," I said softly. "Get him."

Mojo was a sweet dog. He was the kind of dog that would lie on his back for a tummy-rub from strangers in the street … at least, strangers that I was speaking kindly to. But let's face it—he'd had a stressful day. Mojo was only too happy to hear a command to rough someone up a little. He launched himself, snarling and snapping and looking like a holy terror, at the middle-aged guy with the bald head and the full beard. The guy, of course, had no idea that snarling and snapping was as far as Mojo was likely prepared to go in terms of an attack. He jumped away from that bike as if he'd been shocked, hands up in the air like he was trying to persuade the cops not to shoot.

Not much in the mood for conversation, I just got on the bike with Mojo, balancing the huge duffel on my back. Then we took off to find a quiet place to bed down. Because, as of that moment, I was officially exhausted.

Chapter Ten

Mallory

The funny thing is that, back at the apartment I never really was a great sleeper. I'd try different things, like going to bed earlier and setting my alarm to wake up early. And going to bed late and sleeping later in the morning. Exercise in the morning. Exercise at night. Fast at night. Eat at night. No matter what, I spent restless nights staring at the clock and feeling like the only person in the city who was still awake.

But at that makeshift campsite that Joshua set up, I slept like the dead. Maybe it was because the dead had been chasing me all day long, but I slept harder than I remember having slept for ages. You'd think I'd have had horrible nightmares. But, despite the situation and what really was a pretty grim outlook, I felt safe.

When I woke up, Joshua had already gotten up. His white hair stood around his head like a halo in the gentle breeze. He'd even made a small fire, waving the smoke away with a book as it burned—I guess so that it wouldn't alert anyone, living or dead, to our presence. Over the fire he'd taken some of the bread from the car and the ready-to-eat bacon I'd thrown in and made toast and bacon.

He spotted me coming out of the tent and gave me an apologetic smile. "I would have trapped something, but it sounded like you weren't really at the point where you were ready to eat fresh meat yet."

I nodded wryly at him. "That day will, unfortunately, probably come. But for right now, eating out of the car is all right with me. Thanks, Joshua."

We ate in a companionable silence, the sounds of the woods making a peaceful background noise for us. Finally, I said, "Joshua, this is none of my business and you can remind me of that." I hesitated. "It's just that—well, I was wondering—it's just that you seem so organized and knowledgeable."

Joshua gave me an understanding smile. "You mean, how did I end up being homeless? It's okay, don't worry. Your question is only natural. And it's one that I've asked myself many times. If I'm knowledgeable, as you say, it's because I've really honed my survival skills as a homeless person. But how did I *end up* this way? It all really comes down to one single thing: bad decisions. That must be hard for you to understand, since you seem to be a very professional person who probably doesn't have much experience with poor decisions."

I shook my head. "On the contrary, I made a really bad decision less than a year ago. I got in a toxic relationship with someone—a relationship that was bad for me in every way. Everyone could see it but me. Somehow I either *couldn't* see it, or just couldn't own up to the fact that I'd made a mistake."

"Stubborn?" asked Joshua.

"And how."

"That's something we both have in common, then," said Joshua, carefully cleaning up the napkins and the paper plates that we'd used and putting them in a makeshift trash bag. "I'm exactly the same way. And, like you, I made bad relationship decisions. I also made bad decisions in every other aspect of my life, too. I wasn't a good father. I couldn't stop drinking, even though it kept me from holding down a job or being a good husband or parent. Plus, I stubbornly refused to seek help or even acknowledge there was a problem to begin with."

I sighed. "If I'd only paid attention sooner and realized that I wasn't in a healthy relationship."

Joshua said kindly, "But the big difference between us is that you didn't allow your bad decision to continue impacting your life. You said that it was less than a year ago. In my case, my bad decisions compounded and impacted my life and my family's lives for decades."

"But you seem well now," I probed.

"Lack of funds can definitely help contribute to sobriety," he said, his eyes twinkling. "I think you need to pat yourself on the back for having the strength to get out of your situation instead of beating yourself up about it."

He finished putting the small fire out as I enjoyed its remaining warmth. Suddenly I was reluctant to leave this basic campsite. The unknown out there seemed very ... unknown. "I don't suppose we could just stay here for a while?" I asked. I reddened after I asked, feeling a little silly. "I mean, it seems really quiet here and peaceful. Safe somehow."

Joshua said softly, "But your friends are waiting for you, aren't they? Won't they worry if you don't show up soon?"

They would. They definitely would. But after the terror of yesterday, seeing people who had started out as innocent victims themselves turn into vicious killers, I hung back.

"I understand why you'd want to stay here. There

is water nearby. And there are animals we could trap. Plus, it's very quiet," said Joshua.

I nodded. So where was the downside?

"The only problem here is that we're totally exposed," he continued. "There isn't any type of shed or abandoned building that we can stay in for protection. And the water supply, although it's decent, may not always last if we don't get regular rainfall."

"It's just a temporary solution, then," I said, disappointed.

"It would be better if we had land we could farm, too. Eating a diet of game meat would probably get old after a while," he said, eyes twinkling. "It's very shady here and the soil is rocky. It's not a great place to farm."

I took a deep breath. "I guess we should head for Annie's and Jim's place. That was probably the best plan all along. I know they keep a garden there. And it's still very remote. I think they even have a well or something."

Joshua's face grew serious. "One thing that we do need to take care of is getting gasoline. I noticed that you weren't exactly sitting at a full tank."

I suddenly wished I could just go lie back down again. My head was throbbing. "Right, it's only got about a quarter of a tank. And the car drinks gas down pretty fast. There's no way that's going to last until we get to their house." Then I remembered something else. "I don't even *exactly* know where I'm going. I know the general direction, but we're probably going to have to hunt around the house a little while, since it's been about a year since I've been there. I meant to use my GPS to get an exact location, but I got distracted."

I got distracted by helping Joshua, actually.

Although I was glad I did. I'd have been completely nerve-wracked if I'd been out here in the woods by myself. I'd have been sleeping in my car with the doors locked and jolting awake at every sound.

"Have you tried it? Just to see?" he asked.

I doubted I would be able to pick up a signal, but I pulled my phone out. And sighed. "Battery is dead. I've got a car charger, so we'll put it on the charger and maybe we can try again when we're getting gas for the car. I do know how to get there most of the way It's just when we get to the final leg that I'm not sure about the turns we need to make."

I was still weirdly reluctant to leave. I say it's *weird* because at work I'm always a take-charge person. All day long I say, "I'm on it," when the senator asks me to do something. I'm an action-oriented person. It's not like me to linger or procrastinate. But I had this tremendous reluctance to face the world again after escaping it so thoroughly.

Joshua somehow seemed to understand. "I'll help you scout out a place to stop for gas," he said. "I know I wasn't much help yesterday with the nap I took." His expression was chagrined.

"I just admired you for being able to nap, under the circumstances," I said with a grin.

He returned the smile. "Today will be different. I'll be a real copilot. We'll get you to your friends' house."

"We'll get *us* to my friends' house," I corrected. And he smiled again at me.

Fortunately, we were still in a rural area for the next thirty minutes we drove. At that point, I don't think I could have handled another city and another crowd of soulless eyes gazing hungrily at me. The rural areas seemed naturally safer, less-populated, less-likely to have huge numbers of used-to-be-humans around.

But thirty minutes later, we were in dire need of gas. And the rural route highway wasn't offering any places to stop. I got the feeling that Joshua was biting his tongue, wanting me to reach a particular conclusion myself. Eventually, I did. "I guess we're going to have to get onto the interstate and then exit off." The words slouched reluctantly from my mouth.

Joshua's expression was relieved. "Unless you know for sure that there's a small town or a gas station up ahead on this road."

I shook my head.

"We don't want to run out of gas here. This area is more exposed and it might take us a while to get into a heavily wooded section again. Let's connect to the interstate the next time we see a sign for it and then we can fill up and get back on this road again," said Joshua.

A couple of miles up the road there was a sign pointing to the interstate. I couldn't shake this feeling of dread that I'd had since that morning. Still, I took the exit. There were a few cars there, whizzing by at tremendous speed. Fleeing for their lives, I supposed. I had no intention of pushing the accelerator that hard and burning through the small amount of gas we had left.

"I suppose no one's worried about being stopped for speeding," I muttered. "At least the interstate isn't completely backed up. Which is sort of odd, actually. The roads were already jammed back in Raleigh."

Joshua said softly, "Maybe that's as far as the cars could go...Raleigh. Maybe the only cars we're seeing here on the interstate are people escaping from small communities."

It made sense. With everyone fleeing the city at

LIZ CRAIG

once, there were wrecks and complete stops. Those vehicles blocked the exit routes. No wonder they hadn't made it this far. I'd never seen the interstate this quiet. It lent a very eerie feeling to the road. As if it were the middle of the night ... but it was broad daylight.

A few minutes later, Joshua spotted a sign for gas stations at the next exit. "We should probably take it, don't you think?"

I did, since we were probably running the car on fumes. But I didn't feel good about it. I squeezed my hands tightly around the steering wheel.

The station was old, but it at least had digital pumps. I pulled into the station and we peered around cautiously from our locked car. Finally, I figured the coast must be clear and pulled up to a pump, popping my gas door, muttering while fishing around, "I guess it won't let me gas up without swiping a debit card first."

Joshua stopped me. "Let me fill it up."

I hesitated. "Do you think this is a safe station? Should we keep driving?"

"I don't think we really have a choice," he said. "We probably won't know how safe it is until we take a look around the property. Besides, I think it would be a good idea to go inside the station and see if they have a gas can or two. It would be nice to have some extra gas on hand in case there *isn't* a gas station the next time we need to fill up."

"Okay. But are you sure that you want to go inside?" I still couldn't shake that underlying fear.

"It's all right," he said firmly. "This is something I want to do."

Chicken that I was, I was relieved. I was worried Joshua was in danger, but I couldn't be more relieved that I wasn't getting out of the Subaru.

He opened the door and paused for a second. "Mallory, if I tell you to drive on, I need you to drive on."

I started shaking my head immediately. That wasn't part of the deal.

"No, please. If I tell you to leave, or if I'm getting attacked in any way, I *need* to know that you're going to keep going. Keep moving ahead with your plan," he said in an anxious voice.

I reluctantly nodded. "Just be careful."

"I'll fill the tank first, since that's the first priority." He climbed out of the car and quietly closed it. Then he filled up the tank completely, his back to the Subaru the whole time. He gave me a thumbs-up when the gas started pumping. We were both relieved that the pumps were still working, since they ran on electricity and we didn't know what the situation at the power plants was like.

Once he finished pumping, he carefully put the gas cap back on and closed the gas door. Squaring his sloping shoulders, he pulled up to his full height of about five and half feet, and walked to the station.

It was then that I realized I was still clutching the steering wheel with white-knuckles and my heart was pounding so hard that it hurt. I wanted to open the car door to yell at Joshua not to enter, but I was scared to attract those creatures. I sat frozen, mouth dry, staring at the gas station.

Chapter Eleven

Ty

The store looked deserted, but that's the way I always remembered it being. Dad always used to mutter, asking how Bo could stay in business when it was so quiet here. The big thing I remembered from the store was Bo's fondness for country music—the cornier and peppier the better. He'd blast it so loud that I wondered the man was going deaf. Sure enough, as I stepped through the door of the store, the country music was playing away.

One thing I'd worried about was that looters might have come to the store and wiped it out before I'd gotten here. But apparently I shouldn't have worried because the stores were still stocked. This was a place where you could find almost anything—from live bait, to baby chicks, to to old-fashioned candy and soft drinks. The wooden floor sagged and I bet it creaked. That is, if I could have heard the creaking over the country music.

Now all I needed to do was somehow convince Bo that I needed a bunch of stuff from his store. Maybe if I told him that he could put it on credit to Dad? But there was something in me that made me hesitate to call out for him. Where was he? Could he hear the bell ring when I walked through the door? Or was the music really *that* loud?

"Bo?" I called out softly. As I walked and looked around, I felt a tingle up my spine. "Bo?" I reached over and took a baseball ball out of a rack on a shelf. Just in case.

There he was. Directly ahead of me. Leering at me with blank eyes from around a clothes rack. Name on his shirt. Spattered with blood.

He charged me and I swung the bat blindly in front of me. I took a deep breath, focused, and then poised the bat again as I backed toward the door. Bo advanced, moaning softly, stumbling toward me, undeterred by the baseball bat.

That was how the next few minutes went. In slow motion I walked backward to the door, brandishing the bat ahead of me and watching Bo as he kept advancing. When I got outside, I heard the car door open. My eyes still trained on the store owner, I said urgently, "Ginny, stay where you are."

"No, Ty," her voice pleaded with me.

I made my voice as calm and reasonable as I could. I noticed that the zombie in front of me didn't seem to be listening to our conversation at all. Its eyes were trained on me as its mouth worked open and closed. "Ginny, it's okay. He doesn't understand us. Listen, I'm going to lead him away from the store. He's not very fast. I'll head over to the far end of that field and then run back to the store. I'll go in through the front door and lock it behind me. Do you think you can drive the car around to the back of the store? Wherever the back door is."

Ginny's voice shook. "I don't know. I can try."

I backed slowly down the stairs, glancing behind me with each stair I took. "Remember the car is still turned on. So you need to grab the gear stick and move it to *D* for drive and then push real lightly on the accelerator and barely turn the steering wheel. The brake is next to the accelerator. When you're done, you need to move the gear stick back to *P* for park."

I knew Ginny would be frantically trying to remember it all. "Okay, Ty." There was a tremor to her voice, but she sounded determined, too.

I eased away from the staircase and backed toward the large field with Bo stumbling toward me. "Tell you what, why not get started now while I'm here. First, close that car door and crack the window just enough so you can hear me over the motor."

Ginny gently shut the car door so as not to attract attention to herself. Bo still eyed me hungrily. She rolled the window down a little ways and I slowly walked her through putting the car in gear with her foot on the brake (that part was important and I'd forgotten to tell her the first time). I sagged with relief as Ginny eased the car forward.

"That's right, just coast," I said louder since now I was at the field and Ginny was driving away. "Then drive to the back of the store and push slowly on the brake and put the car back in park."

Once Ginny had coasted around to the back of the store and I didn't hear any crashing sounds, I kept focused on Bo and his arms reaching toward me. He didn't look as badly decomposed as you'd think a dead body would look. Maybe he'd just recently gotten infected. That didn't make me feel any better since it meant that maybe other zombies were still hanging around.

Bo lunged at me every now and then so I held the bat in front of me like a lion tamer holding a chair. We continued slowly like this as I backed out across the field until the country store was in the distance. I was conserving my energy for the big sprint.

When I felt like I'd have a strong head start, I bolted toward the country store, running as fast as I could. Bo gave a surprised grunt and started lumbering after me. Panting hard, I glanced back over my shoulder. There was no way on earth that he was going to catch up with me. But that wasn't really what I'd been worried about all along—I really was worried that he'd finally reach me when I was loading up the car with all the stuff from his store. Although I guess it wasn't really *Bo's* store anymore, since it wasn't really *Bo* anymore.

I stumbled up the stairs of the store, looking for a way to lock the door behind me. Bo didn't have a bolt lock, I realized, feeling frantic. Where would he have put his keys for the deadlock? I looked around me, head swinging from side to side. Did he have them on him? My stomach had a sinking sensation.

Finally, I spotted them near the cash register and partially covered by a magazine called *Country Living*. He must have been reading it before he was attacked. I swiped the keys and, hands shaking, locked the deadbolt. I glanced out the window and saw that Bo was about halfway across the distance to the store.

I ran in the storeroom, yanked out some boxes, and started pulling things off the shelves. I skipped the kitschy country stuff and went right for the weapons, which were locked up behind the cash register. And yes, the key was on the same keyring. I grabbed a tomahawk (although I wasn't excited about the idea of getting that close to a zombie), another sleeping bag and tent, a bunch of seeds of different kinds (and here I didn't really know what I was doing, so I hoped the sheer volume would make up for any errors), lighters, a hand-crank flashlight/radio combo, gas cans, and even Ginny's toilet paper for being such a good sport.

I was heading out when I spotted something I didn't recognize and I spared half a second reading the label. When I saw what it was, I smiled and threw it in the box. The only thing I didn't see was water or water purification and that was really our biggest need. I craned my neck, searching high and low, feeling my heart thud in my chest. Finally, I gave up. Bo had returned to the front porch and the sounds of him pounding on the door made my blood run cold.

I didn't even know where the back door was, but I figured there had to be one, right? I hefted the box, shifting it slightly to make it easier to carry. Then I hurried to the back of the store. I saw the storeroom I'd gotten the boxes from, a small restroom, and then I did see another door that looked like it might go outside. I tried it … and an alarm went off. I guess Bo had it tied to the alarm system to prevent shoplifting. My heart jumped into my throat.

I stumbled outside with the box and Ginny was there in the car, face white, eyes huge. I heard the car doors unlock and I ran to the van. Glancing to the side, I saw him at the same moment that Ginny screamed my name. Bo was already around the side of the store, growling fiercely. I was almost to the car when I tripped over a root and went sprawling. A sick feeling came over me as I scrambled up and tried to stuff everything back in the box. "Ginny, lock the car doors!" I yelled.

Bo was almost on me when I heard the car engine rev into life. Ginny must have laid a foot on the accelerator powerfully hard, struck Bo full-on, and he smashed into the wall of the store. He was only stunned, which just went to show how un-human he had become. I focused on the box and my feet this time, taking advantage of Bo's efforts to regroup, and shoved the box in the car. Ginny scooted over into the passenger seat and I jumped in the driver's seat again and we took off.

We rode in silence for a long while as I headed in the direction of our Nana's retirement home. Finally, I hazarded a look at Ginny, scared to see the damage that whole incident had done. But she looked stronger than I thought. There were tears on her cheeks, but her jaw was set in a determined way that I'd seen before. "Thanks, Ginny. I couldn't have driven any better back there than you did. You saved my life."

She gave a choking laugh. "I was paying you back for saving mine at the school." After a few quiet minutes, she asked in a hesitant voice, "Ty? Was Bo nice? I mean, when he was alive?"

That's when I heard the guilt in her voice. This gave me a feeling of relief. I could deal with guilt. I knew how to handle that. If she'd shown signs of some kind of PTSD or something, that's what I wouldn't have known how to handle. "Bo seemed great—when he was alive. But he's not even a person anymore, Ginny, and we had nothing to do with that. You didn't even really hurt him...did you see that?"

She swung her head around to look at me in surprise. "I didn't hurt him? I mean ... I didn't see what happened. I couldn't look at him after I hit him with the car. I just figured that I'd killed him. I *should* have killed him, hitting him that hard."

"You only stunned him. He was just sitting there against the back wall of the store trying to get what remained of his brain together to have another go at me. And you kept that from happening," I said firmly.

I knew then that Ginny had grown up a lot since I picked her up at the middle school. And I wasn't sure it was totally a good thing. I wanted to get her over to

Nana for better parenting than I could provide.

Hoping to get a smile on her face again, I said, "Hey. I got you some toilet paper."

She gave me a sideways look and her eyes twinkled briefly.

Then I remembered the other thing I'd shoved into the box on the way out. "And take a look in the box. There's one other thing in there that I thought you might like. Bo actually had some pretty cool things in there.

Because I'd had to shove things back in the box when I'd fallen, everything was sort of jumbled around and dusty from that red clay that's everywhere in North Carolina. She rummaged around for a minute and pulled out the one thing that she didn't really recognize. Then her face lit up. "A solar-powered iPod charger?" She gave me a huge hug.

If something as small as listening to music could bring down her stress level and make her a kid again? I was glad I swiped it.

Chapter Twelve

Charlie

It wasn't long before carrying a huge pack of looted goods made my back ache. That, and the odd position I was riding the bike in to ensure Mojo was securely on.

Fortunately, I knew a spot that I could temporarily stash the stuff and feel, with any luck, at least a little safe. It was farther from the city, out in a wooded area. It was acres of private property where the family of a friend of a friend of a friend allowed me to hunt some years ago. As I recalled, the area was fairly remote, had a steam running prominently through it, and wasn't close to any large towns, although there were a few nearby houses. The middle of nowhere.

Long term, I sure didn't want to spend the rest of my life hanging out at a primitive campsite with Mojo. I was formulating a not-very-concrete plan that involved Mojo and me driving to another remote location. That one was in Virginia, near the North Carolina border. In fact, it might be that it was in *North Carolina*, near the *Virginia* border. I had a good buddy from school who moved there. I'd visited him every couple of years or so. The house was in an unincorporated town. I figured that meant that there wouldn't be a whole lot of undead wandering around and that I could handle the few undead that *were* wandering around.

Right now, I was just focused on getting completely away from the city and off the interstate. The interstate was still fairly free of heavy traffic and realizing this meant most people hadn't made it out of town tugged at my heart.

I left the interstate and exited onto a secondary highway where there were no cars at all. I drove on that for a while until we came up on the area where I'd been hunting before. I slowed the bike down and then took it off the highway so it wouldn't be seen. Mojo hopped off before I did, since the ride had gotten too bumpy for him and I was going so slow. I stashed the bike in a clump of bushes and snapped my fingers softly to Mojo who bounded behind me as we set off into the woods. Getting the heavy pack off my middle aged back was priority number one.

We trudged deep into the woods until we reached an area near a stream with some flat ground. I took the duffel bag off my back and slung it down with relief. I sat down with my back against a tree and noticed one of my hands was shaking. Typical. I get a case of nerves *after* I've escaped from the zombie apocalypse. Mojo lay against my leg and immediately fell into a heavy sleep. I envied him his ability to just conk out like that. Sleep was probably going to be elusive for me that night.

I fished my cell phone from my pocket, relieved to see the thing still had some charge left. I wasn't sure how great my reception was going to be, and was surprised to find it wasn't too bad. There must have been a cell tower somewhere nearby. I scrolled through my contact list to find the name of my Army buddy. More than anything, I was desperate to find out more about what was going on. I was a nightly news junkie and I always read the paper. I listened to network news. I had CNN on my phone. CNN's website was already down, which was kind of disturbing. Maybe it was just overloaded with traffic?

If there wasn't any official news available, I was willing to get my news straight from a reliable source. I dialed Steve and prayed he'd answer. I thought I might go crazy not knowing the big picture of the epidemic.

I felt a wave of relief when Steve picked right up. "Charlie?" he asked with some surprise. "You okay out there? You …made it out of town?"

My stomach flipped. "Yeah, I made it to a safe place in the woods. Safe right now, anyway. Why? Is Raleigh especially bad?" I knew Raleigh was bad. I knew it when I saw how light the traffic on the interstate was.

"Yeah. Yeah, it is. Good to hear your voice, man. I thought you were a goner, for sure." There was shouting in the background.

I said, "Hey, I know this isn't a good time to talk."

Steve snorted. "There ain't gonna *be* a good time to talk. Besides, the infrastructure is probably going to take a hit soon and this might be our only chance. Figure you're trying to get some inside information, right? I wish I had it. I can tell you that we do not have this thing, this plague, under any kind of control."

My heart sank. "So you haven't been able to cut off and quarantine Raleigh?"

"Raleigh?" Steve's voice was sad. "Dude, it's all over the place. All over the US, anyway. And sure to soon be around the world since people are trying to escape by flying out and then they're turning as soon as the plane goes up. There doesn't seem to be much intel on what this epidemic is and they'd like to put a label on it, since *zombies* don't sound scientific, you know?"

"I know," I said absently. I couldn't get over how fast this was spreading and over different places all at once.

"It's basically some sort of plague that's highly contagious. Most of the time the victims turn immediately, but sometimes it takes a few hours. Nobody knows why. And the ones that *don't* turn immediately are a real problem because they end up becoming part of an uninfected group, turning, and then attacking the uninfected. In our briefing, the brass was saying maybe some sort of disease that's been dormant for a millennium or two and has reawakened. And it's just like the zombie movies you've seen ... shoot 'em in the chest and they just keep coming like a bad horror flick. But if you shoot them in the head? You got 'em."

Good to know. Although I was hoping I could hide out and avoid the whole head shot thing entirely.

"What's the official response been like?" I asked.

"Lousy," said Steve. "The local authorities were all slow to respond today. Overwhelmed. Clueless. Some cities are trying to solve the problem by setting up checkpoints to keep citizens in their towns. This hasn't exactly go over well with uninfected people who are trying to escape. So lots of stories of the police losing it today and gunning down desperate people. The citizens who were forced to stay in the towns felt like sitting ducks. Naturally, this created a panic. People stampeded other people trying to get out. Really awful stuff." His voice was heavy.

"When did the National Guard and the military get called in?" I asked.

"There was delay with that, too. The municipalities were just so shocked by the whole thing that they didn't take the next logical step of immediately calling in the big guns. They should have done that at eight o'clock this morning. Although I'm not sure that we're all that much help. We're too late for containment (which just goes to show how fast this thing is spreading), but we're trying to create safe areas, some camps where it *is* safe. We could quarantine people trying to come in to make sure they're not infected and then we allow those people in."

I said, "Any hope for some kind of immunity or vaccine or something?"

"Nada. And even though it's early, it's such an epidemic that something needs to be developed like yesterday. I guess somebody in a lab somewhere is working on something, but who knows how long that'll take. Hold on." He spent a couple of minutes listening to someone and then barked out orders to another group. "Sorry. Okay, I'm back. But listen, I probably gotta go."

"Just one thing. Is there anywhere I should be heading? Anywhere good to go? Anywhere safe?" I asked.

He sighed. "Knowing you? I'd say head out to the woods and either lay low there for a while or else go somewhere out in the country to a well-fortified house. 'Cause I don't see you meekly hanging around in some camp for rationed food, supplies, and stuff. That would drive you nuts." He broke away to speak to someone again and when he returned to the call, his voice was grim again. "Take care, Charlie. Watch your back." He clicked off.

It sounded worse than I'd hoped. I'd hoped to hear that the epidemic was moving slower. I knew it wasn't, though. Not after that patient turned on me in the ambulance. No, it was spreading fast and it sounded like the authorities today had been slow to contain it. By the time they *did* try to contain it, it was already too late. Now I knew there really wouldn't be a safe spot anywhere. I needed to watch my back in the woods, in rural communities, and anywhere else that Mojo and I went.

My stomach growled and I raised my eyebrows in surprise. Had I been so wrapped up that I hadn't realized how hungry I was? That wasn't like me. When was the last time that I ate? When had Mojo last eaten? The German shepherd opened his eyes and watched me as I rummaged around in the duffel bag. It had been a while since either of us had eaten a meal. I pulled out food from the backpack and offered it to Mojo first. I shook my head in amazement as the dog waited for me to eat first. Like he wanted to make sure that I had something to eat, myself, before he ate what I'd given him. You couldn't beat a dog for loyalty.

After Mojo and I had eaten, exhaustion hit me like a Mack truck. Between first-day-at-work nerves, unexpectedly encountering the zombie apocalypse, and a busy day of looting, I couldn't be tireder. I hesitated. Was it even worth putting the tent up tonight? Trying to figure out new equipment as the sun was rapidly setting? I felt like I was tired enough to crash out in the open on a tarp, so that's all I pulled out of the duffel.

Once I curled up on the tarp near a clump of bushes to keep me from feeling so exposed, Mojo loped over and lay down at my feet: head up and a watchful expression on his face. I realized that while I was sleeping, Mojo was planning on keeping a lookout. I fell asleep with a faint smile on my lips.

Hours later, I woke to growling and sat straight up, heart pounding. For a second, there in the pitch dark, I wasn't sure where I was. Then I remembered and was even more on edge. Mojo's fur stood on end and he emitted a low warning growl as he trained his eyes into the dark distance. There was no moonlight and it couldn't have been darker.

I fervently hoped it was a deer or an opossum or maybe an owl that was worrying Mojo. The dog wasn't used to being outside—he always slept with me at home. Or, at least, he's slept with me since my divorce. My ex-wife wasn't too enamored with sharing a bed with Mojo. Or, actually, with me for that matter.

Although I hoped it was an animal, I felt an overwhelming gut feeling that it wasn't. I didn't think Mojo would be concerned about an animal unless it came right up to us. Mojo was too smart for that. I think he was trying to warn me about something else.

I slowly rose to my knees and then stood up. This had felt like a safe place. It *should* be a safe place. But I knew that my friend's friend's friend's (whatever) family lived here and they had a nearby neighbor. What if the mail carrier had attacked them, or even an infected local cop? It could be anybody. I turned on a flashlight since I couldn't see in the dark as well as Mojo. I wanted to better illuminate whatever danger we might be in. I reached for the duffel bag for the gun I'd loaded last night before going to sleep.

But it was too late. A few yards away now, I could see them. The family who'd graciously invited me to hunt on their land was now prepared to hunt me on it. Their hollow eyes stared hungrily at me and their arms reached out, swiping at the air. They moaned as they came.

Chapter Thirteen

Mallory

Joshua had only been in the gas station for a few minutes, but it felt like hours had gone by. That's because my mouth was so dry and my heart pounded so hard that I felt stress pouring out of me, dragging the time out. Finally, he reemerged from the store, clutching a gas can. His eyes were huge and worried and he waved at me to drive off.

"What?" I asked frantically. I put my window down a little. "Come on, Joshua! Let's just get out of here. We'll find another gas station. This place is creeping me out."

He shook his head and pointed far away, motioning for me to drive off. That's when a guy with hollow eyes wearing a baseball cap and a shirt with his name on it stumbled out of the gas station after Joshua. After Joshua, that is, until he spotted me in my car. Then he lurched in my direction.

I knew Joshua had to be a lot faster than this guy, but he was still frantically motioning at me to go.

"Joshua! Come on! You can make it!" I yelled. I turned the car engine on and slowly coasted away from the slow-moving zombie.

He shook his head sadly at me as I directed the car close to him. "Mallory, I can't."

Undeterred, I stopped the car, unlocked the

passenger door and shoved it open. "Hop in! Hurry!"

He reached over, threw in some gas station snacks and the empty gas can and said, "Sorry I ran out of time to fill the gas can. Mallory, I've been infected already." He raised the arm he'd kept close by his side and I could see it was bloodied. He firmly pushed the lock button. "I can't get into the car with you or else I'll put you in danger. You'll be okay. Leave now!" His voice this time brooked no argument. He slammed the door shut and was dragged away from my car by the zombie in the baseball cap as another lumbered toward him from inside the station.

I finally listened to him. My foot slammed on the accelerator. I was barely able to see where I was going with my tear-soaked eyes. And I was unable to handle looking in the rear-view mirror at the scene behind me.

Later, I realized I'd gotten back on the rural route highway on autopilot. I couldn't remember the miles that I'd driven in that fog I was in. All I could think about was the loss of my odd, kind, friend and how truly alone I was now. As I drove away, I took a few minutes to honor Joshua. Whatever mistakes he'd made in his life, I knew one thing: he was a good, kind man and I was lucky to have had him with me the short time I had.

I drove on for several more minutes before I discovered that I was completely exhausted. There was no way I was going to be able to complete the drive up to the safe house when I felt like this. Despite the fact that I'd had a decent night's sleep. Despite the fact that it wasn't really late in the day. The events at the gas station, which I wouldn't allow myself to revisit in my head, sapped the life from me. I felt numbness coursing through my body. I didn't know if it was a coping mechanism or not, but all I knew was that I didn't really care about much right then except sleep.

But I didn't feel safe. Not like I had last night when I'd drifted off so easily in the woods with Joshua to keep watch over me. The safety aspect wasn't my top priority, though. I just wanted sleep. And that need was pushing me forward.

I wanted something completely familiar. I didn't want to camp out in the woods right now. I wanted a comfortable bed, a nightstand, a clock. I wanted curtains to block out the light, since it was still the middle of the day. I headed once more back on the interstate and drove a couple of miles to an exit that advertised a chain hotel I'd stayed at before. I took the exit. I had no illusions that there would actually be staff at the place, but maybe I could figure out how to get a key to a room. Or maybe the rooms weren't all locked and I could find one and sleep for a while, behind a locked door. I could even try to call Annie and Jim from the hotel phone. Hotels also usually had food, which was something I knew I was eventually going to be interested in, even if I wasn't right now. Maybe I could raid the area where they had their free breakfasts. Or maybe this one even had a full restaurant on the premises.

Driving up, I saw that the hotel looked deserted with only a couple of cars in front. I saw no zombies lurking in the parking lot, which was a good thing since I was in no mood to deal with them and I didn't have any weapons.

I parked my car close to the building and walked in. As expected, there was no one at the front desk. It lent an eerie atmosphere to the hotel. But how was I supposed to get into a room? Did the hotel have those key cards with the magnetic strip, like most hotels?

I walked around the front desk and started opening drawers. I heard voices approaching from the direction of the stairs and I quickly ducked out of site as the door from the stairway opened. These might be people who'd make good allies, but they might be people I needed to avoid. I didn't have the energy to figure out which they were. There were several different voices, maybe two male, one female. The voices passed the desk and went into another room nearby. When I peeked to see where, it was clear they were in the hotel restaurant. As soon as they left my sight, I quickly headed up the stairs, abandoning my quest to figure out how to work the magnetic key card device. That was one thing I did agree with them on ... I wasn't going to trust the elevator. Although there seemed to be electricity now, who knew how long that was going to last?

On the first floor, I peered out of the staircase and looked down the hall to see if any rooms were open. I did see a couple of doors that looked cracked open, instead of closed. But wouldn't most people stay on the first available floor and save themselves the trouble of going all the way up the stairs? I decided, for my purposes, it would make more sense if I kept on going upstairs.

I was huffing and puffing by the time I made it to the third floor. I peered down the hall again, and again saw doors that appeared to be cracked open instead of closed. I walked to the first one and looked in. It looked as if it had been ransacked, and not by the person who'd been a guest here. Someone had gone through their suitcase, pulling out clothes and searching for ... what? Money? Jewelry? Did people still care about material things now?

I felt like Goldilocks as I wandered down the long,

empty hall. Each room I saw was ransacked in the same way. I guess the guests must have left abruptly due to the panic...maybe trying to return home to their loved ones? Trying to return home and collect their things before escaping town? Was the hotel itself attacked by zombies at some point yesterday? Followed by looters?

Finally, I found a room that wasn't ransacked. It wasn't ransacked because it obviously hadn't been occupied. The bed was made up and the room appeared to be awaiting a guest. I decided I would step into that role.

Since the looters (who were perhaps the people downstairs) apparently had a master key to open all the doors, I put the chain on. Then I kicked my shoes off with relief, pulled the covers down, and climbed into the bed. It must have been only seconds before I fell asleep.

I don't know how long I slept, but it must have been a long nap since the light outside was starting to fade as the sun went down. What had awakened me were the voices again. I sat up in the bed, clutching the bedspread. At first I thought I was hearing the voices from outside in the hall. Then I realized they were too muffled and distant for that. They were coming from outside. Then I realized—my things. All of my stuff in the Subaru.

I jumped from the bed and stumbled to the window, pushing aside the curtain to see. Sure enough, there were two men and a woman who were breaking into my car. The worst part was that they were smashing the windows to do it. Those windows had provided at least some protection between me and the zombies. Once they'd broken a window, they reached in and opened up the door, dumping all of my things onto the ground to sort through them.

I was shaking, my hands were fists beside me. What was I going to do, though? I didn't want to confront them, because who knew what they might do? I couldn't call the police. The police were slightly busy right now. I felt totally helpless, completely impotent. It was frustrating and maddening to stand there and watch my remaining possessions be sorted through and carted off. Looting survival equipment and food and water from a store was one thing. That's completely understandable, given the circumstances. But going through someone's personal possessions and stealing money and jewelry … how could anyone think that would benefit them at this point? And they must have realized that my car hadn't been in the parking lot for long. They must know I didn't just abandon it. They were taking advantage of the situation.

They immediately opened and ate food I'd taken from my pantry. There was a big man who appeared to be in charge of the other two. He was pointing at things and barking orders and they were deferential to him. When he pulled out Joshua's modest backpack, I thought I might need to be restrained from running down there and confronting them all.

Which was when I noticed something out of the corner of my eye. From my bird's eye view on the third floor I saw that a group of five zombies who, according to their uniforms, had apparently been workers at this very hotel, were lurching toward the group looting my car. I learned that, as angry as I was over the violation and the selfishness of the looters, I couldn't condemn them to their fates. I pounded on the window. The windows were thickly-paned and I wasn't nearly as loud as I wanted to be. I pounded harder.

The thin woman with them glanced up. Her eyes darted around until she spotted me in the window facing them. She said something to the big man and pointed up at me.

I pointed at the approaching zombies and tried to convey my fear with frantic motions. But the big man misunderstood me and thought I was trying to keep them from rifling through my things. He grinned audaciously at me, holding up a bag of chips and making a show of stuffing several in his mouth. The other two laughed at his antics, ribbing him and ribbing me. I pounded again on the window, making my eyes big, pointing at the zombies who were just on the other side of the car now, but to no avail. And then it was too late. I turned away so I wouldn't have to witness any attack. There was nothing more that I could do. Wearily, I climbed back into the bed.

Chapter Fourteen

Ty

'Ty? Are we going to go see Nana now?"

Ginny sounded exhausted and I knew that I was. It was dark now. The thought of spending the night in the woods wasn't very appealing, but the thought of us trying to figure out if the situation at the retirement community was safe while we were this tired didn't exactly sound like a good idea, either. Besides, I really didn't have much experience driving at night.

"Ginny," I broached carefully, "I want to see Nana too. But it's been a really big day. Right? You were in school this morning and since then we've escaped town, looted a store, and run over a zombie with a car." I tried to get a smile out of her and was glad to see just a hint of one play around Ginny's mouth.

"What are we going to do, though?" asked Ginny. "Where is it safe?"

I was wondering the same thing. "We could go into the woods and camp out—just for tonight. We do have camping equipment."

"Do you know how to put the tents together? Because I don't," said Ginny.

"The one I took from the garage I could put up in my sleep. But it's a one-person tent. The one I just swiped from Bo is a new tent that might take me a while to figure out. And we're losing light pretty quickly, too," I said, trying to think it through.

"Couldn't you just turn on the van's headlights and set up the tents?" asked Ginny.

I grinned at her. "You're thinking pretty well on your feet, Sis! That's a good idea. The only thing is that I just don't know how far this ... infection ... has spread. We might not want to attract any attention to ourselves with lights. Maybe, just for tonight, we can sleep in the van."

Ginny turned in her seat and looked doubtfully into the back. It was a mess, since I'd just flung stuff in the back in a massive hurry. The third row of seats were down and there was camping stuff and food and water bottles all over the place.

"I can move some things around and make a place for you to lie down. And I'll put the seat all the way back and just sleep in the driver's seat," I said.

Ginny reached over and gave me an unexpected hug. "You're doing a great job, Ty. Better than Mom and Dad would have done."

I felt myself coloring at the praise. I muttered, "Not that great of a job."

"You are. You know how Mom and Dad were."

I did. And it didn't escape my notice that she was talking about them in the past tense. In a lot of ways, that was probably healthy.

I carefully drove the van off the road and through a break in the trees off the rural route highway. I was hoping to conceal it a little from the road so that no one would see us, but vans aren't exactly good off-road vehicles. Moving the stuff around did take a little longer than I thought. But by the time she and I closed our eyes, we were completely exhausted. I fell asleep quickly to the almost immediate sounds of Ginny's regular breathing as she fell into a deep sleep.

I woke up the next morning jerking out of my sleep with a gasp. Life itself was a nightmare right now, and waking up, my situation didn't seem any better than it had in the dream. I checked my watch and saw it was already noon. We'd been tireder than I'd thought. Ginny was still sleeping and I hated waking her up. Maybe I could just start driving and she'd still be able to catch up on sleep.

I needed to use the restroom, though. I smiled at my choice of words. Restroom. Yeah, there weren't too many of those around. I didn't want Ginny to wake up and not find anyone here, so I gently moved to the back of the van and lightly touched her shoulder. She woke with a start, too, just like I had.

"Hey, it's okay," I said. Lying to her, as usual. Things were pretty far from okay. "It's morning, but you can keep sleeping. I just needed to let you know I was going into the woods for a bathroom run."

Ginny's brow crinkled. "Okay. I need to go, too. But I hate going in the woods."

"Not many restrooms around here, Ginny." I shrugged.

"No, I don't mean that. I just mean that it's kind of … it's scary in the woods." She said the words with hesitation, like she thought I might laugh at her. But I was far from finding anything humorous right now.

"Tell you what. When I come back, I'll just hang out on the edge of the woods in earshot and you can go, okay?"

She nodded, eyes drooping again sleepily.

"Maybe you can even go back to sleep while I'm driving to Nana's," I said lightly.

Ginny smiled at the mention of Nana. "She always has treats for us. Peppermints. And she makes that great pound cake. Do you think she can cook for us? It's been a long time since we've visited."

I was just hoping she hadn't been run out of the place. That she was still there. That I could offload some of this huge responsibility I had to an adult who was related to us. "Sure. You know how much Nana loves cooking for us. And she has a kitchenette on her hall." And she might even have total run of the big kitchen, too, depending on whether the staff deserted them or stayed.

I headed off into the woods after making sure that Ginny had locked the van doors after us. Now that it was daylight, the van was a lot more visible than it had been at night and I was ready to get out of there.

I hadn't gone far into the woods when I heard a soft groaning approaching behind me. My breath caught and I whipped my head around. It was a group of zombies. In fact, it looked like an entire family. A dad in a denim button-down shirt, a mom wearing a cheerful floral dress. Even a little girl in a Disney shirt and a toddler boy wearing overalls. Their eyes were hollow as they gaped at me.

I started backing off. They were slow, I reminded myself. Much slower than I was. But the woods were full of obstacles and I was outnumbered four to one.

The dad clumsily made a swiping motion at me and I scurried back a little. "Ginny!" I called out loudly. "Drive away!" There was no answer and I wasn't sure she could hear me. Had she gone back to sleep?

My heart sank as I heard a rustling behind me. I turned to see another zombie staring at me. That's when I jogged away, heading deeper into the woods. They grunted and jogged awkwardly after me, a good deal faster than Bo had been, but not as fast as me. I stumbled over a root but caught myself before I fell.

I couldn't seem to shake them. They didn't tire. They just blindly headed for me, loping behind me, training hollow eyes on me the whole time. The scariest thing was that they looked so harmless if you didn't see their faces. And that they were so hard to shake off.

I finally stopped panicking and started thinking. It took a while and I was pretty far into the woods at this point. They weren't fast. They *were* really awkward and hardly sure-footed. I spotted a steep, rocky hill covered with roots. I took a deep breath and sprinted up it and then down the other side. Sure enough, I could hear them muttering and groaning to themselves as they tripped over themselves and the hill. I didn't wait around. I ran as hard and as fast as I could back in the direction of the van. I was so glad I'd left the keys with Ginny. Maybe she drove away. Or maybe I diverted all of the zombies in the area away from her.

My lungs felt as if they were bursting. Running in unfamiliar terrain wasn't easy and I winced as my ankle turned going over a root. But I kept going, heading straight for the direction that I knew the van had to be in.

And it wasn't there. I looked frantically around me. But this had been where it was, I was sure of it. I looked for tire tracks but it had been too dry to leave any. There was no grass in that area to tamp down. But the bushes looked like they'd been crushed down—was that from the zombie family stumbling through, or from the van?

I ran down the road, up a hill, looking for the van, peering into the woods to see if I'd just gotten the area wrong. But there was no sign of the van anywhere. I ran back the other way, craning my head, listening in the silence for the sound of the van's engine rattling. But I saw nothing anywhere. How long had I been gone? It felt in some ways like hours, but I knew it must only have been about twenty-five or thirty minutes that I'd been chased and run back. Did Ginny run into zombies, herself? Or was I in totally the wrong spot? The woods all looked the same. There weren't any real identifying factors. And I hadn't exactly been looking for landmarks when I left. I'd never thought I wouldn't be able to find my way back to the van. It has completely disappeared.

I kept going—far in one direction and then turning around and going far into the other. The light coming through the trees played tricks on me, the shadows sometimes looking like a human figure. Sometimes like a lurking zombie. But nowhere, nowhere did I see the van.

I heard gunfire not too far off and suddenly realized how exposed I was there on the road. I headed into the woods again on shaky legs. No Ginny. No van. And, while I was adding up the things I *didn't* have, I now had to add food and water to the list.

I did have my cell phone in my pocket. It was almost out of power. Mom and Dad hadn't let Ginny get a cell phone yet, so I couldn't try to reach her that way. But I needed so badly right then to hear a friendly voice. I kept trudging into the woods until I found an area with lots of trees and bushes to shield me. I took out my phone, pulled up my contact list, and started dialing.

The phone rang and rang. Finally, an answering machine picked up. "Hi!" said a chirpy voice. "I can't come to the phone right now, so leave a message and I'll get back to you just as soon as I can!"

When the machine beeped I said, "Nana? Nana, it's Ty. I don't know if you're okay or not. Listen, I might not have a battery on my phone for long. Mom and Dad?" I swallowed. "Nana, I'm sorry, but they're gone. Ginny and I are okay. At least, Ginny *was* okay, but now she's missing and I'm not in a great spot. I just wanted to let you know that she and I are going to try to reach you. So maybe look out for us? I need help. And ... I love you, Nana."

Even though I knew it wasn't a good idea, I kept calling her machine after that. Not enough to run my phone battery down much, but just to give me a boost. I couldn't feel lower than I did right then.

After I finally stopped calling Nana, I sat for a few minutes, trying to figure out what I should do. I decided I had a few priorities. I needed to find Ginny. I needed to find water...the running had made me super-thirsty. And third was that I needed to find some kind of weapon. Rocks, a big stick...something. Even if it wasn't really effective against whoever or whatever my enemy was. Until then, I was going to feel really exposed and helpless and that wasn't the way I wanted to feel.

I started walking, trying not to make much noise. I wasn't sure how the zombies found us last time, but I wondered if sounds drew them. It would make sense. They were hunting, after all.

When I stopped panicking and finally started thinking, I stopped feeling like I was going in circles. I still hadn't found Ginny or any sign at all of her, but I did see narrow trails where animals had traveled. Figuring there had to be some water nearby, I followed the trail until I found a shallow creek. I didn't have any water purification equipment and I didn't feel real good about making a fire to boil the water, either.

That might attack zombies too—I didn't want to risk it. So I just knelt down by the stream and cupped my hands and drank my fill. I might pay the price later, but for right now, that water was the best stuff I'd ever put in my mouth.

I walked the whole day. To keep from being too exposed, I'd hike through the woods and then peer out onto the road at different sections and scan the area for the van. Sometimes parts of the woods all looked the same, but I tried to make sure that I was systematically covering the area. The problem was that I wasn't sure if Ginny had driven the van *forward* and parked, or if she'd made a turn and gone in the other direction.

I found rocks and put them in a pile in a concealed, wooded area that I thought might make a good place to bed down that night. I found a couple of heavy sticks and put them by the rocks. Simple weapons, but they made me feel better than not having anything. I even found some trash in the woods that I rinsed out in the creek and filled with water. No sign of Ginny anywhere.

When the sun started going down, my heart sank with it. Where was Ginny now? It was getting dark. Was she safe? Was she scared?

When it was totally dark, I crawled into the bushes where I'd stockpiled the homemade weapons and water and lay down. There was nothing to do but sleep. I stared at the stars through the branches, counting as many as I could see to distract myself and to try to relax enough to actually be able to sleep.

Finally, I must have fallen asleep, because the next thing I knew, I woke to the sound of twigs snapping and a panting sound. My eyes flew open to see a pair of glowing eyes.

Chapter Fifteen

Charlie

It was, indeed, an entire zombie family. Although it was hard to look at them, they resembled the family that were friends of my friends and owned this land we'd hunted on. They looked extremely normal and suburban until you realized the infection had made them lose their humanity.

"Mojo!" I cried out. He was in full defense mode. He gave commanding, deep-throated barks and snapped his jaws at the air in front of them, backing off quickly as they reached for him before barking and snapping again. When I called him, he looked back at me with a pleading look in his eyes. It was a sort of: *I've got this, boss. You go! Go!*

I didn't pay attention to his doggy sign language. Instead I tried to get him back. That's right: at that moment, fighting zombies seemed like a better idea than offering Mojo up to them. I aimed the gun and managed the calm precision to pick off the dad. Unconcerned by the fallen zombie, the other zombies turned their attention away from Mojo and trained it on me again. "Mojo! Run! Run!" I yelled.

He threw me a frustrated look. This wasn't what he wanted. As the zombies lumbered toward me, he made a large loop around and then did this dodge and retreat move that was intended to herd them away from me. He snarled at them and snapped at the air in front of him with his impressive row of teeth. Somehow, although I wouldn't have thought the zombies would be afraid of much, they seemed intimidated, backing away, hissing at the dog.

The mother zombie abruptly stumbled away and the zombie children followed. I called Mojo, but he wasn't satisfied and continued herding them away into the black night. He apparently *would not* be satisfied until they were out of sight. Maybe even farther away than that. Who knew the dog was such a perfectionist?

Finally, he was satisfied and returned to me, panting. I poured some water from our supply (making a note to myself that I needed to filter and refill at the creek later today) into a folding bowl. He lapped it all up and then lay down beside me, still looking watchful.

Once again, I fell asleep...a testament to my exhaustion. And once again, I woke in the pitch black darkness to growling from Mojo. The difference was that this time Mojo was far away from me. He apparently had some kind of perimeter in mind that the zombies couldn't cross. And I guess they had.

"Mojo!" I yelled, struggling to wake up. I cursed, fumbling for my gun and getting to my feet.

But Mojo was determined. I never could see him, never could see what he was guarding me against. I could only assume it was a zombie. If it wasn't, it must have been some other night creature. Whatever it was, I could only hear Mojo's snarling and barking as he advanced into the woods. And I felt totally helpless for the first time since this had started. Maybe I should have swiped night vision goggles because Mojo had a huge advantage in that he could *smell* the danger, but he could also *see* it in the dark. And whatever he'd seen, he was chasing after it.

I stood there, conflicted. I wasn't sure how much help I'd be for him out in the dark. Wouldn't he come back to our campsite? The dog was so smart, I was sure he'd be able to find it again.

So I waited. It felt like forever. What was more, it started raining just enough to give me a chill. I reached in the duffel and pulled out a windbreaker, yanking it up around my shoulders and zipping it up. A light breeze started up, which made things even cooler. There again, though, Mojo had an advantage with his fur coat. The cool rain probably felt refreshing to him.

I was wide awake now, not about to drop off to sleep. I waited for what must have been an hour. I couldn't hear or see Mojo at all. Once I gave a piercing whistle, hoping to bring him back. When I realized what *other* creatures might be attracted by sound, I decided to hold off on any more whistling.

When dawn was just starting to make the terrain a little lighter, I put a canteen on my belt loop, took my gun, and set off to look for my dog. Even then I felt like any zombie could hear me coming a mile away as I stumbled over roots and sticks and rocks as I scanned for Mojo or signs that he'd made his way through.

And I saw and heard nothing. Apparently, I was making so much racket coming through the woods that I was even scaring normal wildlife because I saw no raccoons, no birds, no opossums.

After walking for over an hour, and with the light now pretty good, I saw a house in front of me. It was indeed the house of the family that had hosted me when I hunted here years before. And I figured it must also be the house belonging to the zombie family. It was a modest ranch-style house with a small garden off to the side and some riding toys scattered around in the yard. Seeing the toys made me feel a swift sadness for the zombie kids I'd seen. They were victims after all. I took a moment to remember them as they had been before their attack, when they'd just been hosts to me on a hunting trip. Because I couldn't spare any sympathy on them in their current state.

I drew closer to the house and hid behind a tree as I studied it. The back of the house had no curtains at all and there were lights on inside so I could see in. I guess the residents had found their house private enough to forgo curtains or blinds. It sure was good to see that electricity was still working.

I saw no signs of activity at all in the house or the yard so I slipped up to the back door and listened for a moment. No sounds came from inside. The family must still be roaming the woods, looking for food. *Their* kind of food, since there appeared to be a perfectly good meal still sitting abandoned on their kitchen table. Had they been attacked at mealtime? I felt a pang as I thought about Mojo. Maybe I could scavenge more food for us while I was in here. I might be able to put up more of a search when I had some food in me, too. I locked the door behind me.

I did a quick check around the house to ensure there wouldn't be any surprises. The family were excellent housekeepers and the whole place was exceedingly tidy to the point where I had to stop myself from taking my shoes off as I walked around their house. I pulled open the large closet door in the master bedroom and let my breath out with relief when I saw there was nothing in there. I checked the other rooms. Nothing in the closets. No cats hiding under the beds, waiting to jump out at me. The doors and windows were all locked. I started to relax for the first time since day before yesterday when this whole thing started. There was a picture of the family in the den—sure enough, it was the zombie family that had attacked Mojo and me. Except, in the picture, they looked happy and normal.

I headed into their kitchen first. I felt bad for a minute eating their food. I had to remind myself that the family didn't need this food anymore—that this wasn't what they were interested in. I opened their fridge, figuring I should eat the perishable stuff first and possibly leave with some of the cans from their pantry. I pulled out a couple of yogurts and a block of cheese, then I found an open box of crackers and a bowl of fruit on the counter. I felt like a large, filthy Goldilocks through the entire process and could only hope the three bears didn't show up while I was here.

Of course I was still hungry. I'd been fighting for my life for the last couple of days and a Frenchified meal of fruit and cheese wasn't exactly going to fill me up. I returned to the fridge again, this time mentally prepared that whatever was in the fridge was mine for the taking. The zombie family owed me that, at the very least, for trying to kill me, right?

This time I decided I was in more of a breakfast mood, since it was dawn and all. I took out eggs, shredded cheese, bacon bits, and a sliced onion. I found a large skillet under the stove and cooked an omelet for myself. I only wished Mojo was here so that he could share my feast with me. I promised myself that I'd find him.

After I finally had enough to eat (in the short term, anyway), I poured myself a tall glass of sweet tea from a pitcher in their fridge and set out to get cleaned up and use a real restroom. This was second on my wish list—hygiene. There were neatly folded fluffy towels under the sink in the master bathroom, which I pulled out. I even made use of their fruity smelling shampoos and bath products, although I knew I might regret it later when the mosquitoes came by to check out who smelled so exquisite.

It was a long, long shower, I'm not going to kid you. I really wasn't sure how long the utilities would last in our new and dangerous world, so I took full advantage of them while I could.

When I finally got out of the shower and stepped out into the steamy bathroom vanity area, I decided that I really, really didn't want to put on those dirty clothes again. I tried to remember how big the zombie husband was. It had been a while since I'd stayed here. Of course, when I'd seen him today, he'd looked like he was ten feet tall and three hundred pounds to me. That was just because he was terrifying me by coming after me. But realistically, he was probably about my size: around six feet tall and fairly lean and muscular. The guy seemed to do a lot of work outside the house and was in pretty good shape. I decided to check his closet and drawers. I found he was *slightly* bigger than me, but that I could make it work because we wore about the same size jeans.

It was a testament to how quickly life had changed that I really didn't even feel odd about wearing this guy's clothes. In fact, the clothes felt awesome because they were so clean. I pulled out a few extra things to take with me to the campsite, before pausing. Wouldn't *this* place make more sense to hide out in than the open campsite? I'd be a lot less exposed, especially if (and I felt a huge pang at the thought) Mojo weren't there to keep an eye out for me. Yes, I could effectively get *trapped* in this house if it were surrounded by zombies, but really, how many zombies could there really be in this neck of the woods?

I decided to hang out long enough to see if the newly-minted zombies viewed their former home as sort of a home base. Were they, in their infected state, not even cognizant of their old life? Their home? If that was the case, I thought that holing up here, at least for a while, might be a good thing.

I walked into their den again, wincing at the family photos. I turned on their television to see if I could find some news. The first station was completely off the air. The next station was running old movies and old shows—I guess it had been scheduled to play before the crisis started. The next couple of stations had nothing, either.

Finally I found a local channel playing news, but it wasn't the sleek type of news show that used to run. The anchor had more of a ten o'clock shadow than a five o'clock one, and his jacket and tie were nowhere in sight. He didn't seem to be *reading* the news either, which is what anchors usually do. In some ways, this looked like an old fashioned newscast—the kind where somebody would come up to the news desk with updates on sheets of paper. Which is exactly what happened.

The bearded anchor quickly glanced over the paper and his face grew even more grim. His voice was hoarse and breaking by constant reporting. "We have a report from a source in the military from our national bureau who states that efforts to contain the impact of the virus to specific areas has been unsuccessful. As you may know, martial law was implemented soon after authorities realized the virus was spreading rampantly and after the CDC reported that a possible cure may be a year or more in the making. However, again, the efforts to contain the virus to specific areas has failed. Once again, authorities are directing citizens to specific shelters that the military is guarding."

I saw a list of shelters running at the bottom of the screen just like the list of school closings that sometimes ran during ice storms in the winter. It looked like the military had commandeered a local school and a local hospital, among other locations. But what was their longterm plan? What were they going to do when the place got overcrowded or the swell of zombies outside was too much for them to handle? When they ran out of food and water? No thanks. I thought I'd just take my chances *outside* the shelter where I wasn't fighting with my fellow humans for supplies.

The anchor continued, "If you're just joining us, here's a quick recap. Currently, we're getting reports of widespread panic in areas where the virus is spreading. People are desperate to get away and are basically clogging up freeways and other escape routes in their efforts to escape their communities. Authorities recommend that fleeing residents should instead head for the nearest shelter as escape routes are difficult or impossible to navigate due to these traffic jams. We do have reports of some individuals holing up in their homes and defending themselves with stockpiles of weapons, some of which may have been looted in the immediate aftermath of the start of the infection. The police have confirmed that they unfortunately do not have the resources to respond to every call for assistance. Authorities, however, do not recommend that citizens remain in their homes since it doesn't offer a longterm solution."

Unless you were out in the country. As I was. Fewer zombies to defend against, although they were clearly still here.

"Although currently some areas do still have power and other utilities, there are already reports of scattered outages. A spokesman from the power company stressed that these utilities were dependent on human monitoring to keep working. It is expected that, in time, the utilities will no longer be available to citizens. The spokesman reiterated what the authorities have been urging: that residents should, when they can safely do so, travel to one of the official shelters set up by the military, in order to stay abreast of developments and to receive supplies."

Still didn't sound appealing. And when the anchor started repeating much of what he'd already said, I turned off the television. Clearly they didn't have any other news. I wasn't really sure what I'd hoped to hear when I tuned in. That the CDC had invented a vaccine in, what? The last three days? That the authorities had found a weapon that eliminated the zombies and were gaining the upper hand? I snorted at my optimism.

The only really good news was that the zombies hadn't returned to the house. I made one more check to make sure all the doors and windows were locked and then I lay down in an impossibly tidy room that surely must have been a guest room. Little did they know the type of guest they'd be hosting or the circumstances their hosting would fall under. I figured if I could just get some solid sleep, maybe I could plan clearer. I set the alarm on the clock radio that was on the nightstand next to me and quickly fell asleep.

When I woke up, once again I wasn't sure where I

was. But at least this time I was comfortable, although my body was tense and fragments of a nightmare were popping in and out of my mind.

And then I realized the source of the nightmare as I heard groaning and scratching outside the house.

It appeared that my zombie family had returned from their travels. Or, to continue my analogy, the three bears had returned to find Goldilocks sleeping in their bed. Did they know I was here, though? How would they? It's not like humans have fantastic sense of smell and on some level they *were* still human. No, maybe they were just trying to get back into a familiar place. In which case, maybe this wasn't the best location to bed down, after all.

I lay frozen in the bed. After a few minutes of listening, I realized that these zombies, besides being very slow, were also not endowed with superhuman strength. Which made a lot of sense. Why would what was basically a corpse suddenly be as strong as Superman?

The zombies also couldn't seem to *reason* their way into the house. They weren't using rocks to smash the window in. This was oddly comforting.

The only problem, then, with these infected people, was that they seemed to be on track to vastly outnumber the rest of us. And that *was* a problem. They weren't fast, they weren't smart, and they weren't stronger than us. But there were scores of them and they were determined hunters.

I decided that I'd take a few things with me in a backpack that I'd found in the master bedroom closet. I might very well return, but I didn't think I wanted to return *today*. I would find Mojo first, and if we came back here and those zombies were hanging around, I didn't think Mojo would take it very well. And I wasn't in the mood to chase after him for the second time in a day.

I stuffed in some of the husband's clothing, canned goods and bottled waters, and then cautiously peeked out one of the windows. It was a window on the end of the ranch house where I thought I could see what was going on without being close enough to have them see *me*.

Sure enough, there was the happy family, scratching repeatedly on the back door of the house that led to the garden. They appeared strangely intent on their scratching.

Since they didn't seem able to work entry to the house out, I decided I should lock the front door after me once I'd slipped out of the house. I searched for the keys. After all, it seemed as if this family was attacked at home, right? So both sets of keys should be floating around.

Finally I found a set—very neatly hanging on a key holder near the garage door. But the garage door was, I felt, too close to the zombies at the back door. So I walked to the front door, peeked outside just to be sure there were no more undead lurking around, and then carefully locked the front door behind me.

I didn't want to pass within view of the zombie family at all, so I took a long route around them. I headed to the portion of the woods that was directly ahead of the front door, although that wasn't the direction I wanted to go in. But it would give me an opportunity to search for Mojo and keep me covered by the brush, as well.

I decided that Mojo had probably just headed back to our makeshift campsite. That seemed very much like something a dog would do—get back to where the stuff was and just wait for his owner. At least I hoped like heck that was what he was doing. I wanted my dog back.

After twenty minutes of walking with no sign of Mojo, I was finally in the section of the woods where I needed to be … the section directly behind the back door of the zombie house. I squinted over and saw the zombie family still scratching with determination at their back door.

I walked and walked. I was heading generally in the direction of the campsite, but I was also taking short detours from time to time to see if I could find Mojo along the way. That dog had such an attuned sense of hearing, that if we was in earshot, I was sure he could hear me coming, no matter how quiet I might be trying to be.

There was no sign of him anywhere. As I walked closer to the site, I felt my neck and shoulders bunching up with tension. Was he at the site? Was he okay?

I stopped dead when I reached the site. Because it *was* the site. That I knew for a fact. You could even see the bent grass where I'd slept. But the duffel bag and all my stuff was gone. And there was no sign of Mojo.

Chapter Sixteen

Mallory

When I woke up this time, I knew exactly where I was and what was going on. I was in a hotel. I'd just watched my car basically get rendered unusable by looters. My few possessions were strewn around a parking lot populated by roaming zombies. I felt numb. But I also felt refreshed. I squinted at the clock and saw that I'd been able to sleep a couple of hours

Still, I lay in the bed. I stared at the ceiling as I tried to figure out what my next move should be. Staying at this hotel was definitely not a good longterm solution. There were obviously zombies in the area. I still had a tough time thinking of those infected victims as zombies, but it certainly made it easier than thinking of them in a sympathetic way as former moms, husbands, and children.

In the short term, I decided I needed to take advantage of the amenities that I did have. I needed to get cleaned up. I needed to see how much food those looters had left in the hotel. Then I needed to get away. The problem part of the whole plan was the getaway. I didn't much like the idea of driving a car that had broken windows. Not with zombies trying to get in. So maybe I needed to find another vehicle, although even thinking about taking someone else's car made me feel like a thief. From what I could tell, though, I was the only living inhabitant of the hotel. It was dead silent in the building and the front desk certainly hadn't been manned. The uniformed zombies that attacked the looters must have been the front desk staff for the hotel and they clearly wouldn't be needing their keys or their cars any longer. I rooted around behind the front desk to see if I could locate any keys.

Next I would need to recover as much of my stuff as possible from the parking lot and throw it into the "new" car while eluding zombies.

Maybe I needed to check and see if the mini-bar in my room was stocked.

My entire plan both scared me to death and made me very determined and focused. I did have a tiny bit of beer (because who knew the next time a cold beer might come my way?) from the mini-bar while I took a hot bath and got completely clean for the first time in days.

Then I headed downstairs to check out the 'complimentary breakfast' area. Usually it would just have cereal boxes, milk, eggs, sausages, oatmeal packets, coffee, and things like that. It looked like the looters had eaten up a good amount of the breakfast foods that had been put out by the staff so I went down a short hall to see if I could find a pantry or a storage area where the hotel kept its food. Bingo. And it looked like the looters hadn't made it that far. They'd probably been too busy trying to find rooms to break into.

The hotel front door wasn't secured and, upon quick inspection, didn't seem to really be able to *be* easily secured. I guess that made sense, since when the business was operating normally, people likely would have been coming and going at all hours. But it didn't make me feel safe. I pulled out a clean, clear garbage bag from a box in the storage room and put as many items as I could in it. Making sure the coast was clear, I took the bag up to "my room," which I'd been careful to leave unlocked so that I could get back in if I needed to. I was so paranoid by this time that I even checked around the hotel room and bathroom to make sure there were no looters, no zombies, or just anything I didn't know about in there before carefully bolting the door behind me. Being on the run like this must have done something to my mind.

I sat down at the desk in the room and started opening cereal boxes. I ended up eating a lot more food than I thought I would. I hadn't even realized I was hungry before I started eating. I didn't even want to think about how much sugar I was downing as I kept going through cereal boxes. Ordinarily, my diet would have been something I spent more time considering. Right now, I was just glad to have something to eat that I didn't have to catch or grow myself. Because, if Joshua was right, that was going to be the next step.

After I finished, I stood up from the desk and pushed the curtains very gently aside to peer out. A quick check satisfied me that, as of right this second, there were no zombies wandering around near my car. My caution with the curtains made me wonder again if I was starting to lose it. I knew that these zombies were probably not staking out the hotel and looking for movement inside, but...maybe they were. I didn't know anything at all about these things and I wasn't sure where I could find any source of information. I remembered that an area downstairs near the lobby did have a couple of computers for travelers to check their email. I wondered if I felt brave enough to sit down there with my back to the room and try to find news stories on this epidemic.

There was always my computer, but I was guessing that was probably one of the things the looters flung from my car. I squinted across the parking lot. There was something black peeking out from underneath a quilt my grandmother made in a parking space next to my car. I had a feeling it was my laptop. And laptops didn't do so well when they were flung onto asphalt.

Belatedly, I remembered my phone. Maybe I could find out some information by pulling up a news site. When I fished it out of my purse, though, I saw it was completely dead. That's when discouragement set in. It was bad enough being alone. It was even worse being alone with no information about a frightening epidemic. Were there safe places to go? How widespread was the problem? Could I book a plane to Canada? Would they even let me in, or were they protecting their borders? Was Annie okay? Did I even have a shot at making it to their haven in the middle of nowhere? Were there zombies in the middle of nowhere?

Then I had a brainstorm. Surely there were chargers in some of these rooms. Right? Or maybe even at the front desk. I could take a charger, charge up my phone while sitting in a locked room, and check the news before ... well—basically before stealing a car and trying to leave with at least some of my stuff.

I picked up my garbage bag of food, unlocked my door, and poked my head out. I saw no one and heard nothing from any of the rooms. I figured this probably wasn't the best hall to find a charger on—the whole reason I'd chosen it, after all, was because it looked like no one had really been staying here. I headed down the staircase and back down to the second floor, peeking out the door to look down the hall. Again, I heard nothing and saw nothing. The eeriness of the empty hotel was scary in itself. I felt as if I were in a ghost town.

The first room that was open and had been inhabited by a guest didn't have the right kind of charger for my phone. It took me a while to even find the charger because the looters had flipped the suitcase and I'd had to dig through the contents.

The second room had a charger plugged in. The charger had tape on it, as if the cord had some kind of a short. I figured beggars couldn't be choosers. It looked too fragile to be able to successfully moved so I decided to do my charging in this room. I locked the door and used the chain, just to be on the safe side. I carefully put my phone on the charger, making sure it was charging before walking away from it.

The view was different from this window and I froze as I looked out—zombies. The perspective showed me a different section of the parking lot and gave me the opportunity to see it a lot closer, too, since I was on the second floor. I spotted the hotel employees in their uniforms right away. Now I also saw the looters—they were zombies themselves. I shivered. There were also about ten other zombies, wearing regular clothes, that I didn't recognize. They must be guests. Maybe one of them even owned the broken charger I was using for my phone.

They were milling around, pacing back and forth in the parking lot. They didn't seem interested in coming into the hotel. Maybe they realized on some level that they'd already cleared it of guests … one way or another. I hoped that some of the hotel guests had been able to get away. They must be looking for victims because they appeared to be scanning the parking lot, lurching forward and back as they went. I studied them. Some were in better shape than others. Some I'd have to look twice to even notice that they weren't normal people. Aside from the fact that they were hanging out with a gang of zombies, there wasn't too much about them to set them apart. A vacant expression in their eyes. A slack mouth. That was about it.

I watched them for about an hour as my phone charged. They were moving as a group and I was relieved when they slowly started heading down the road a little. Maybe they had given up on the hotel as a source of food.

I checked my phone. If the zombies were walking away, I wanted to take advantage of it. My phone was mostly charged. Quickly I pulled up CNN. The site was obviously overloaded, or else the connection here at the hotel was really bad. It was taking forever to load. Finally I gave up and pulled up a local news website to see if it would load any faster and was relieved when it popped up after just a short delay. The stories looked as if they'd been written on the fly, with no eye for editing at all. I skipped over the typos and the formatting and skimmed the text. My heart sank. It wasn't just here. It wasn't just the east coast. It looked as if it were spreading all over the United States and there were even early reports of the epidemic spreading into Mexico and Canada. It was going to go worldwide. There was probably nowhere safe to go.

The site also mentioned some shelters that were available and being guarded by National Guard troops and other military. Somehow, though, I just didn't see myself going there. It was bound to be crowded. There were bound to be rationed supplies. I hated feeling trapped and was such an introvert that the idea of spending months or even years with wall to wall people wasn't appealing.

I tried phoning Annie. No answer. I tried Jim. The same. I tried not to think what this might mean. Their phones were probably dead, just as mine had been.

I took the phone and slipped it into my pocket. A few minutes later, I picked up the garbage bag, slung it over my back, and hurried down the stairs.

I walked behind the front desk and started opening drawers. Had the hotel employees kept their keys in here? I didn't see any on the desk and I had the feeling that the looters had likely gone through any purses that were around. I said a quick prayer that the employees didn't have their car keys in their pockets. There was no way I'd try to get them that way.

Finally I found a box on a shelf where apparently female employees kept their purses out of sight. I rifled through and found a key fob on a chain of keys in a black leather purse. The logo on the fob was Honda. Now I just had to figure out which Honda went with the key.

I headed out around the front desk. I caught some movement out of the corner of my eye and stifled a gasp as I dropped out of sight behind the desk. My heart pounded. Had they seen me?

I peered out from behind the desk slowly and saw a small figure with long, brown hair walking away from me. A child...a little girl. Waves of relief coursed over me. I stood up and was about to call out to her when she turned around and stared at me—with vacant eyes and a slack mouth. And moaned.

Pity, revulsion, and fear made me shake. I

grabbed my garbage bag of food, clutched my key in a suddenly-sweaty hand, and took off for the front door. No time for subterfuge now. I'd planned on carefully stealing around the parking lot, trying the key on every Honda while watching my back and listening for noises. Now I was going to have to hit the alarm button on the key fob and make a run for the car as fast as I could. I had the bad feeling that the sound of the alarm was going to attract the band of zombies to me.

Either way, it was my only choice. I hit the car alarm as soon as my feet hit the parking lot. Right now, I wasn't going to have time to get my things. A means of escape was the most important thing. I heard the alarm coming from the back of the hotel and ran harder. It made sense that the hotel employees would park the farthest away, but it sure wasn't helping.

I hazarded a glance behind me. The zombie girl was far behind me, but the group of former hotel employees and looters was heading my way faster. I stumbled, recovered my footing, and ran harder to the car with the blaring alarm.

I yanked the car door open, slid in, and locked the doors behind me with only about thirty seconds to spare before the zombies were at the Honda, pounding on it with the palms of their hands.

I fumbled with the keys for a moment before starting the car, putting it immediately into reverse, and pushing the accelerator hard. I felt like I was back at the apartment once more, trying to escape. Clearly, parking lots weren't the best place to be. I sped out of the hotel parking lot, leaving the zombies stumbling after me.

But I didn't go far this time. I drove down the road

to a location just out of sight of the hotel... it was a big, empty parking lot with a boarded-up big-box store. There shouldn't be any zombies here. I waited for about forty-five minutes there before driving slowly back to the hotel, searching for signs of the group of zombies. Seeing no one, I parked right behind the Subaru, hopped out of the car, and proceeded to throw as many of my belongings into the Honda as possible. I might have been more selective with what I kept and what I discarded this time, except I felt that there wasn't enough time to pick and choose. I kept an eye out the whole time. When I thought I heard shuffling and moaning sounds, I stopped what I was doing, hopped back in the car, and left. Sure enough, the group was on its way toward me.

I'd had enough of the urban experience for now, I decided. The problem was that there were too many infected around. I needed to join up with Annie and Jim, safe in their getaway cabin in the middle of nowhere with the garden and the well. That was the plan. Enough deviation.

I drove out again to the rural highway to head toward the North Carolina/Virginia border. The highway was a somewhat poorly maintained two-lane road with woods bordering each side. I'd gone a few miles when I hit the brakes. There was a little girl with a blonde braid walking on the side of the road. Remembering the horror at the hotel, my hands gripped the wheel. But then she turned to look behind her and I saw the tears on her face and the frantic look in her eyes and I pulled right over.

I put the window down. "Do you need help?" I called. Of course she did. Didn't we all?

She nodded, studying me carefully as to make sure I was someone safe. Apparently deciding that I was, she said, "Can you help me?"

I knew I wanted to. "What's your name?" I asked.

"Ginny."

Chapter Seventeen

Ty

I gasped, flinging myself backward away from the glowing eyes. But as I pushed away from the creature, I backed into a tree that was behind me. I closed my eyes, half-sobbing, waiting for the attack.

And felt a large tongue licking my face.

I reached up with my hand and felt a furry body. A big one. I wished I had a flashlight, some way to really see. And someone must have read my mind because at that moment the moon came out from behind the clouds and shone down on a large German shepherd who was giving me dog kisses.

Relief flooded me and I put my face down in the dog's fur and finally let the tears fall that I'd been holding back the last couple of days. It was so good not to be alone. Being so completely alone … that was what was tough to handle.

The dog must have felt alone too, because it curled itself around my back. I lay down again, this time a lot more relaxed, and fell asleep.

The first light of dawn woke me and I smiled before I even opened my eyes. I could feel the dog's fur against me as I woke up. It sat right up when I did, grinning at me in its dog way. I spotted a collar and reached out.

"Mojo?" I asked him and he wagged his tail to confirm it. So this was someone's pet. Had Mojo's owner turned into a zombie? Or had he just gotten separated from him?

"Hey buddy," I crooned and the dog instantly lay on its back for a tummy rub. *This* was a sweet dog. The only problem was that I had no idea how I was going to feed it. Or myself. Besides being worried sick over Ginny, I was also worried sick over the fact that the van with all of my supplies in it was gone. Right now I had a couple of homemade weapons and some water. That was everything I had in the world right now. I felt that wave of responsibility wash over me again now that I had another living creature to look out for again.

Somehow my tension must have been picked up on by Mojo. He sat up and regarded me solemnly with his amber eyes. "I don't have any food for you," I told him. "But I know where water is. What happened to your owner, boy?"

Mojo kept staring at me. But he seemed sad, his head hanging.

"Here's what we're going to do. I'm going to have a breakfast of water. Then I'm going to see if I can find my sister, Ginny." I suddenly wished I had something with Ginny's scent on it. Weren't German shepherds the type of breed that were search and rescues? Maybe somehow I could get Mojo to at least listen or look out for people, in general. With his big ears, long nose and large eyes, he was like a surveillance super-animal.

Mojo leapt to his feet, ran off a yard or two and gave a short, sharp bark as he turned around to stare at me.

He was obviously trying to get me to follow him.

His eyes were intent on me, totally focused on getting me to follow him.

"Okay, boy," I breathed. "I'm coming. Do you know where Ginny is? Do you?" It seemed totally unlikely, unbelievable. But he definitely wanted me to follow him for *something*. And it wasn't like I couldn't look for Ginny along the way to wherever we were heading. I picked up my stick and a rock to take with me, although now I felt a lot safer with a big dog on my side. I left the water, hoping we could find our way back to the campsite later. Every once in a while, I took the rock and notched a tree.

We walked for what seemed like forever. Long enough for me to wish that we'd brought water with us. Mojo was surefooted and determined, pacing himself so that I could follow him ... sometimes stopping to wait for me to catch up as he led the way. Finally, after we'd been walking for what felt like a few hours, walking through the woods and then looking out on the road for the van, and with no sign of Ginny, Mojo sprinted ahead of me, running to one spot and giving another bark.

Panting a little myself, I hurried up to join him. I felt momentary disappointment that whatever he'd led me to, it clearly wasn't Ginny. But then I saw what he *had* led me to, and I felt excitement course through me.

It was a duffel bag and a makeshift campsite.

"Is this where your owner was, boy?" I gave a quick look around to make sure that his owner wasn't anywhere around—especially in zombie form. I wasn't sure what happened to Mojo's owner, but I sure didn't want to tangle with him.

I knelt down and unzipped the duffel. And stared. Whoever Mojo's owner was, he was organized and smart. Or he used to be, if he was a zombie now. I saw water filters, MREs, camping and hunting supplies, and other things that I needed to survive out here. I put my arms around Mojo and hugged him. His long tail beat the hard, dusty ground in response.

I added some water to two MREs and gave Mojo one. He gobbled it up quickly after making sure that I had something to eat, myself, and didn't want what I'd given him.

It was amazing how a little food could give you a different perspective on life. "Let's go, boy. Let's go find Ginny." I picked up the duffel bag and slung it over my shoulder. It was very heavy and bulky, so it was a good thing I was as tall as I was. I walked off a little ways, and then turned and whistled to Mojo. He was strangely reluctant to leave. He sat at the spot where the duffel bag had been, staring at me for a minute.

"Come on, Mojo. I can't stay here and I want to take the stuff with us. We'll come back later and see if we can find your owner." Although I wasn't real sure I wanted to meet up with him at all. Reluctantly, Mojo followed.

The day warmed up quickly with scorching sun. The woods provided some shade for us, but it was still so hot that Mojo and I kept stopping for water. I used the filter from the duffel bag to make the creek water hopefully safer for me to drink. Mojo just lapped it up straight from the source, of course.

I kept looking for Ginny and I felt more and more frantic the longer we walked with no sign of her. She couldn't have just disappeared. She might have driven a little ways with the van, but she wouldn't have kept going. At some point, she'd have parked it and probably either stayed put in the van or gone looking for me. I needed to make sure she wasn't here in the woods before I tried to find her on the road.

As I was coming up a ridge, Mojo started growling and the hair on his back stood up on end. I dropped back down out of sight again. Although I hadn't seen or heard anything, I knew I trusted Mojo's senses much more than my own. I waited for a minute and then slowly crept along on my stomach to peer over the crest of the ridge.

It was that zombie family again and a chill went up my spine. Then I realized they weren't looking in my direction at all. They were aimlessly wandering in the opposite direction, stopping ever so often to listen or sniff the air. Just seeing that little girl in the Disney princess shirt and the little guy in overalls made my flesh crawl. But I was so incredibly relieved that I didn't see Ginny with them. I'd had this awful worry that Ginny might have been attacked by the zombie family and then become part of their pack. But she was still nowhere to be found.

The frustrating thing was that the zombies were hanging out in the area. I was frozen, waiting for them to move on. Mojo clearly understood the danger and didn't make a sound, lying silently next to me on the hill. Once I had an overwhelming desire to sneeze, but I somehow managed to resist it.

Finally, after what must have been a couple of hours of total tension for Mojo and me, the zombie family started moving off in a very specific direction. It was weird ... almost like they knew there was either food out there or somewhere they needed to be. I was just glad to see them go so that I could finish my painstaking process of maneuvering through the woods and then peeking out at the road.

After a while, the sun set and I realized that I

wasn't going to finish searching today. Especially when I heard the heat of the day firing up thunderstorms. I found a spot under some rocky overhang for Mojo and me to wait out the storm. But all I could think about was how Ginny was so afraid of storms and how worried she had to be.

Mojo was looking pretty worried himself. Before he huddled next to me under the rock, it had been harder to motivate him to follow me. He'd been hanging back and, when I'd turn to call him, he'd look behind him meaningfully.

"Okay. I get it, boy. I told you we'd get back to the campsite. But I can't make it back there today. It's already getting dark and I can't see at night as well as you do. And we don't need to be walking under trees in a thunderstorm, anyway."

These last words were accompanied by a quick, illuminating flash of lightning followed immediately by a crack of thunder that told me the storm must be right on top of us.

The rocky spot felt safe but uncomfortable. We were getting wet and muddy and I shivered.

When the sun went down, the storms finally started lifting. I gave Mojo a rub and said, "Let's set up camp. Just for tonight."

I pulled out a tarp from the duffel bag and spread it on a flat spot of muddy ground. I could see stars above, so I knew it was clearing, and I decided to pass on using the tent that night. Plus there was the fact that I didn't much like the idea of being confined to a tent and not being able to see what might be waiting to attack me. I lay on the tarp next to Mojo, who was still staring alertly into the dark, and closed my eyes.

LIZ CRAIG

The next time I opened my eyes, it was bright outside. I woke with an alarmed feeling, like I'd overslept or something. I pushed myself to a sitting position and then realized why I must have woken up. Mojo was standing, looking with intense focus deeper into the woods. He seemed to be listening with all of his might.

At least he wasn't growling. Not yet, anyway.

I could hear rustling sounds of someone walking through the bushes. I kept watching Mojo. He was tense, but his fur was lying down on his back. It didn't *sound* like the moaning, stumbling zombie family to me. The thought occurred to me that maybe it was Ginny looking for me.

Suddenly, Mojo gave a short bark and then bounded ahead. He wasn't charging ... he was just running.

And then I heard a man's voice filled with total joy. "Mojo! Smart boy! You found me!"

Mojo ran to me and gave his owner a quick bark.

I saw a man come through the bushes, a frown crinkling his forehead. He was probably in his mid-thirties with dark hair and a wiry, muscular build. Nice looking. His brown eyes flickered a little as he saw his duffel bag and the tarp I'd been lying on. He tilted his head to one side, raised his eyebrows, and said, "Wasn't enough to steal my supplies, you had to swipe my dog, too?"

I froze and felt the color drain from my face.

The man gave a quick cry and said, "A bad joke. Sorry. It was more like you were looking out for Mojo while I was gone. And I'm glad you could use the stuff." He reached out his hand and, after pausing a second, I shook it.

"I'm Charlie Black," he said briskly. I liked that he

talked to me like I was a peer of his, instead of talking down to me. "Good to meet you."

Chapter Eighteen

Charlie

Despite the circumstances, this was turning out to be one of the best days ever. I got my dog back and the stuff that was going to help me survive. And this kid was super-impressive. I never like talking down to kids because I still remember how much I hated it, myself, when I was that age. But it was especially easy to treat Ty like an adult because he was behaving a lot more mature than some of the forty year old guys I knew. And he was only a teenager.

The first thing I wanted to do, though, was to eat. And it was time for the kid to eat, too, since he was just waking up and it was the middle of the day. I decided we'd just tap into the supplies for now, although later on I was going to want to hunt so I didn't have to deplete the store we had.

We prepared a couple of breakfast MREs and gave Mojo some food, too. The kid was finally starting to look more relaxed.

"So, Ty. What's your story? Did you take off for the woods like I did, or are you from around here?" For a second, a feeling of discomfort came over me when I realized that maybe he was even the oldest child of that zombie family. I hoped not.

He shook his head and looked down at the pouch of food he was eating. Despite whatever he'd gone through, you could tell he was a kid who cared about his appearance. He had sandy-blond hair that was long on top and flopped over his eyes so I couldn't see them right now. He had dimples that I'd seen flash exactly once when Mojo had begged for food. He was also very tall and lean. Taller than me, actually, with that slightly awkward bearing of a teen that wasn't used to his own size yet.

"It was supposed to be just a temporary thing. I'm from Raleigh," he said. "I'm taking care of my younger sister, Ginny. I pulled her out of her middle school when I heard about the attacks. We got separated when these zombies came up and now I can't find her."

I studied him. Like I said, I don't like talking down to kids, especially teens. But clearly this wasn't a guy old enough to be looking after a younger sibling on a normal basis. It wasn't like he was nineteen or twenty or anything. He must have been more like fifteen ... maybe sixteen. I decided not to ask about the parents. There was no way there could be a good story there.

"That's really cool, to be looking after your little sis like that," I said lightly, instead.

For a second, I thought I saw tears glint in his green eyes before he leaned forward and let the hair flop over them again, hiding. "Yeah, but I didn't do such a great job. Seeing as how I lost her and everything."

"Hey, man, you just had to get away from zombies, right? You weren't going to be any help to her as a zombie, were you? You did the right thing."

And whatever guilt he must have been wracked with seemed eased in that moment and he looked up briefly to give me a grateful look.

"We were in good shape," he said, like he was

mulling it over. "I'd taken the minivan."

"Ooh," I muttered. "Gas guzzler."

"Yeah, that was the bad part about the van. But we had some gas with us and it was good that we could put the seats down and sleep in the back. It made Ginny feel safer, I think," he said.

He was still amazing me every second. Here was a teen boy actually thinking about *what his little sister might feel*. I don't think I wasted a minute at that age thinking about my sister.

"I'd stopped by this country store and loaded up on supplies that I thought we might need. We had food and water and weapons and survival gear. I felt like we were in pretty good shape in the short term," said Ty, like he was thinking it through.

"So you were breaking up your trip, then? Just taking a break as you were moving through the area?"

I could tell Ty was feeling guilty about everything that had happened. "I was totally exhausted and it was dark. I wasn't used to driving the car at night, so I was worried about that. We felt a little safer in the van, so I parked on the side of the road as far off as I could. I hoped nobody would notice us. We had a good night's sleep. I just got out of the van to use the bathroom and ran into zombies in the woods. When I got back to the place where the van had been, Ginny and the van were gone."

His voice broke a little on the end of the sentence and not because it was changing, either.

I nodded thoughtfully. I felt pretty sure I couldn't make much of this situation better for Ty. The chances that his sister was even alive were remote. He'd lost his parents ... at least, that's what I was assuming. But I did feel like I could make his guilt better and at least help make a plan for him.

"Here's the deal, Ty. You went out of your way to help your sister." Ty started shaking his head. "No, no, you did. You could have just decided that the school knew best and that they'd be able to take care of her. But you pulled her out of the school like any mom or dad would." I saw Ty swallow hard at the mention of his parents, and then I hurried on. "You thought it through. Your head was screwed on right, even though you must have been freaking out. You got supplies. You were a responsible driver and got off the road when you realized you were probably dangerously tired and encountering darkness, which was a driving condition you weren't used to. You were attacked—which wasn't your fault—and then you've been tirelessly trying to find your sister ever since. You couldn't have done any more," I said firmly.

He glanced up at me with shimmering eyes before putting his head back down again.

I cleared my throat. "In the interest of knowing what kind of trouble we're dealing with, who exactly were these zombies that you were tangling with? Was it, perchance, a zombie family? A mom, dad, and kids?"

He looked at me again, nodding. "That's the one. Did you see them, too?"

"I sure did. I'd even met them when they *weren't* zombies, which makes the whole thing even worse," I said with a sigh. "Real disturbing. I stayed in their house last night and raided their fridge. I locked the doors to keep them out and swiped their keys, so we could go there and stay tonight, if you want. After we look for Ginny today, of course."

His expression was conflicted. "I like the idea of being in a house. But I feel like I need to maybe keep moving and find Ginny. If we finish looking through the woods and the road today, maybe I need to head for the retirement home?"

"Retirement home?" I asked.

"That's where we were headed. My grandmother lives there and I was thinking it might be a good place for us to be, at least for a little while. It's in a remote area and there is plenty of food and medical supplies there. It's also gated—they have some residents that have problems with their memory, so the place is pretty secure."

I was getting the idea and I had to agree that it sounded ideal. At least for a short stay, maybe even longterm. "I'm not saying it couldn't happen, Ty, but I can't really picture how Ginny is supposed to be getting there. So, you left her with the car, right? And Ginny is … what? Eleven or twelve?"

He nodded.

"Do you think that someone came up and hijacked the car?" I asked slowly.

Ty was resistant to thinking about his sister in trouble and I totally got that. And thought even more of him for it.

Ty said, "No, I think Ginny took off in the car. At the country store I'd given her a driving lesson so that she could get herself out of trouble if she needed to. She even ran down a zombie there."

There was pride in his voice as he explained what had happened at the store. As I was listening, though, I couldn't help thinking that there was a big difference between driving for a few yards and driving off down a rural highway to find a retirement home. Big difference. But I wasn't going to share this with him. It looked like this whole scenario was what he was pinning all his hopes on.

"Tell you what. Why don't we finish up what you

were doing and make sure that Ginny isn't on the perimeter of the woods. Then we can get out of here—get you over to see your grandmother."

Ty nodded, but I could tell he was worried. "It's still a ways away, though. And now I don't have the van. It would take us forever to walk there."

"You didn't steal *all* my stuff," I said in sort of a cocky voice. "I've got a bike."

His frown deepened. "Even with a bike, it might take a lot of time. And I'd hate to take your bike from you."

"No, I mean a *motorcycle*. The only problem is that there's not a whole lot of room, especially with Mojo sitting on there," I said.

His eyes widened. "Mojo rides the bike, too?"

"He sure does. Well, to the best of his ability. He gets the general idea—that he needs to stay on. I kind of curl myself around him to help keep him stable." I was quiet for a minute, thinking. "Do you know who doesn't need a car right now? That zombie family. And, considering the fact that they were obviously at home when they were … uh … zombified, I have a feeling there's a vehicle in their garage, although I didn't look. The key ring I've got does have a car key on it. Even if it's not the right key, I do know how to hot-wire cars."

Ty lifted his eyebrows.

"It's a useful skill," I said modestly.

"Sounds perfect. Then I can lead you and Mojo to the retirement home. If you don't mind coming along," said Ty.

"I don't really have anything else on my agenda," I said in a light voice. It was good to see the kid sounding a bit more upbeat, more hopeful. "Now, the only obstacle to our whole entire plan is one tiny thing—the zombies."

"Is that all?" Ty smiled.

"That's right. Although I've made some discoveries about these undead friends of ours. They don't analyze data very well. As a matter of fact, their decision-making skills are quite lacking. And they're decidedly on the slow side, in terms of movement. What's more, they appear to be attracted by sound." I counted my scientific findings on my fingers. "The zombie family was hanging out around the house when I left it, but with a diversion, I'm sure we can grab the car. Do you think you're up for a diversion?"

"I've already done it once or twice," said Ty.

Finishing the search didn't take long. There was no sign of Ty's kid sister anywhere. We walked back to the zombie house. Although I wasn't fat before, I was already starting to be a lot fitter than I'd been. Ty was mostly quiet, still having a lot on his mind. I'm usually quiet myself, but to help keep his spirits up, I continued bantering in a low voice until we got close to the house. Then I zipped my lips. If the zombies heard us coming, that wouldn't help anything. From the edge of the woods, we crouched in the bushes to look at the house.

"I don't see them now," I murmured. "They might be on the other side of the house."

"Shouldn't they have had *two* cars?" asked Ty. "If both parents were there, I mean. At my house, I had to choose the van because I couldn't get to my dad's car in the driveway." His expression turned bleak again.

"That would make sense, but there isn't a car outside and that garage is strictly a one-car garage. Maybe their car was at the shop or something.

Besides, I'm happy with the bike, so we don't need two cars." I pulled the keys to the house out of my pocket. "Okay, I'm heading in. Just stay hidden unless you see them. Even if you *do* see them, I can slip out the back if they're at the front of the house. Diversions are the last resort, right?"

Ty nodded.

I took a deep breath and jogged up to the house.

Chapter Nineteen

Mallory

Ginny looked terrified, but I must have seemed safe enough for her to hazard getting in the car with me. I unlocked the doors and she climbed in. She was wearing denim shorts and a pink tee shirt and for the life of me I couldn't tell how old she was.

"You're safe now," I told her, sounding confident although the truth was that I wasn't sure. "You're welcome to stay with me as long as you want. I'm on my way to a safe place—a house near the North Carolina/Virginia border."

Her eyebrows drew together as she tried absorbing this.

I continued. "I have friends there and we can join them. They grow their own food and they're in a very, very quiet area so there shouldn't be too many people there. Or no people there." I was starting to drive away again.

Her expression was alarmed. "But I can't leave here. Not for good. I've lost my brother and I've got to find him."

I'd been wondering what a small girl like Ginny had been doing out on her own. It sounded like she hadn't really been on her own at all. "Your brother? Is he in the area?" I parked the car in a hurry on the side of the road because it looked like Ginny was going to jump out of the car if I didn't stop moving.

"He's Ty. He's fifteen. He rescued me from my middle school and had loaded a van full of our stuff." Her voice started getting choked up, so I gave her a minute.

"What kinds of things did he have in the van?" I asked, trying to let her regain her composure on the easy questions.

"Stuff to make water safe. Food. Weapons. We were in good shape. But he had to go use the restroom, so he went into the woods and told me to just stay put. Then these zombies came up and they were chasing Ty farther into the woods. He was yelling back at me to stay put."

I nodded, looking down at my hands, which were folded in my lap. I didn't want her to see the truth in my eyes. The truth that her brother probably hadn't made it. That we really, really needed to get out of this area, especially if there were zombies close by. But I was going to let her tell her story first, before I started persuading her to leave with me.

"So you were alone in the van?" I asked. "Stuck, right? Did you ... did you leave the van to run away? Is it around here somewhere?"

Ginny shook her head. "I wasn't really stuck because Ty showed me how to drive. Not great driving, but enough to be able to get away if I needed to." She stared out the car window at the woods as if Ty were going to show up at any second.

I said gently, "He sounds like an awesome big brother. What happened to the van, then? Did you drive off with it? Did it maybe ... well, did it get wrecked?" Because if I'd been trying to drive a car at her age, I'd have wrecked, for sure.

"No. I waited, instead. The zombies were after Ty,

they weren't after me. So I was sitting in the passenger seat with the doors locked and staring at the woods. Really scared. Then on the other side of the car, there was a knock on the window. Men were standing there and they had guns." She swallowed hard.

Now I wasn't really sure if I wanted to hear the rest of this story. This little girl was precious. I fervently hoped no harm had come to her. "Did they see you?"

"They did." She took a deep breath. "They told me to unlock the doors and open them and I did. Then they argued over me. One of the men kept grinning at me and he wanted to bring me with them." She shivered.

"But the others didn't?"

"The one who did want me was the man who got behind the wheel and started driving off down the road. So I'm not real close to where Ty and I were. One of the men didn't really care either way whether I was with them, but the third man was like the leader of the group or something. He didn't want me to come along because it was going to make more work or trouble for them. I was so glad when they just told me to get out of the van. Then they left. With all our stuff. The van, the food, the water, everything." A lone tear trickled down Ginny's face and she didn't bother to brush it away.

"So they're gone. Like, long gone, right?" I asked. I didn't like our chances against a group of armed men. Again, I felt that urge to start driving away with Ginny as fast as I could to the border with Virginia.

Ginny shrugged. "I guess so. They stopped and let me out and then took off. They were leaving pretty fast. There was a …Mom had left a CD in the van. It was ABBA. They had the windows down and they were playing the music as loud as they could and whooping and hollering." Her face was more stoic now, even though I saw another tear join the first one.

"Your Mom and Dad. They ... you were separated from them?"

"My brother said they didn't make it." She looked gravely at me.

"And your brother ... Ty ... he didn't come back?"

"He's still in the woods," said Ginny in a matter-of-fact voice.

I really wasn't wild about hunting in the woods for Ginny's brother. In all likelihood, he had suffered the same fate as Ginny's parents. That meant, if we *did* find him, we'd be running away from him at top speed. And how devastating would *that* be for the poor girl? But I wasn't sure I was going to be able to persuade her to leave. And there was no way I was going to leave this child here. I felt an instant pull toward her, an instant connection.

"How about this?" I asked, slowly. "How about if we call for Ty for a few minutes and satisfy ourselves that he's not close by? Then ... well, where were y'all heading? Was there somewhere Ty was trying to get to? Because maybe he found a ride, too."

I could tell Ginny felt really torn. "I just don't want to leave him here. He came and got me from school and everything. But I guess we could go to Nana's. That's where we were heading. Maybe that would be the best place to meet up."

I listened carefully to her as she was working through it. Then I nodded thoughtfully. "I think you're right. The woods go on for miles and miles and you said Ty was being chased pretty far in. Then you were driven away from where you started out. So we could search and search and miss him. He sounds like a very smart kid. And a resourceful one. He would think to try to meet up with you at your Nana's house." If he was in full possession of his mind, that is.

"It's not really a house: it's a retirement home," she said. She was quiet for a few minutes and I didn't speak either.

Finally she said, "I want to look for him for a few minutes at least. I can't just drive away. Can we just walk through the woods for a little while?"

"Of course we can," I said, stifling a sigh. "But we can't be too loud. I think these zombies are attracted to noise. So let's *look*. And maybe we can call him really quietly. And if we see a zombie, run as fast as we can."

I pulled the car off the road. Actually, I was able to pull it into the woods pretty far, despite the tree cover. If there were bands of men roaming around and stealing cars and supplies, I didn't want to be the next victim.

We set off into the woods. Ginny's face was hopeful and apprehensive. I wasn't looking forward to the moment when her hopeful attitude was completely dashed. She walked slightly ahead of me, head turning from side to side as she searched for her brother. I took up the rear and was looking for any lurching figures that *weren't* her brother. Occasionally, we'd stop and she'd call out softly.

We saw no one and nothing until about thirty minutes into our walk. The sun was going down and I was started to feel uneasy. That's when a ramshackle shack came into view. It had what looked to be a galvanized metal roof with tattered curtains hanging in the window.

Ginny was staring at the shack as though it were

a castle. "This is the kind of place that Ty might try to hole up in," she said, breathless from our hurried walk through the woods.

I wasn't so sure. This was a guy who had pilfered a lot of camping equipment and then headed into the woods. I was thinking that the great outdoors wasn't really a problem for him. And the shack looked ominous somehow. Like a cottage in the woods in a fairy tale. You always knew something bad was going to happen in those cottages. A witch was going to try to put you in an oven or a wolf was going to imitate your grandmother and try to gobble you up.

I was still staring at the cottage through the dim light and sizing it up when Ginny gasped and grabbed my arm. A zombie stood not even thirty yards away from us at the edge of the woods. She was an older woman in a long floral dress that had seen better days and her gray hair hung wildly around her face. She had a slack mouth and her eyes were staring at us with hungry determination.

"Come on, Ginny, let's go," I said forcefully.

But Ginny seemed somehow frozen in her tracks. I pulled at her arm. She was a small girl, but she was too heavy by far for me to pick up and run through the woods with.

"Ginny!" I urged, loudly now.

The disheveled zombie lurched toward us, reaching out an arm for Ginny. I grabbed Ginny around her waist, yanking her violently and then pushed her in front of me until she stumbled forward. Not fast enough, I knew.

That's when a shot rang out. I automatically ducked my head and so did Ginny, even in the state she was in. The report was authoritative and ringing and I turned fearfully to see the zombie woman was on the ground, no longer moving and eyes staring blankly at the darkening sky.

"Ginny, it's dead," I said. Not that it had really been alive before. "Come on, let's go." Because there was someone with a gun out there and I wasn't sure if we were going to be the next targets.

Ginny whispered, "Maybe the shooter has seen Ty. Can we ask him?"

I really wanted nothing to do with the gunman, whoever he was. I wasn't even sure I knew where the shot had come from. I scanned the area until I spotted the gun poking through a barely cracked window in the shack.

I called out, "Thank you!" toward the gun.

There was no response. The whole thing was making me jittery—the body on the ground, the attack, the gun, the creepy shack in the middle of the woods. The fact that it was now getting very dark. I was ready to leave.

But Ginny called out this time, "Have you seen my brother? He's a teenage boy. He was the one taking care of me."

The gun was pulled out of the window. Then there was a pause before a gruff voice said, "No. Go away."

"You heard the man," I said. I started moving away.

Ginny didn't follow. Instead, she moved closer to the shack. She looked like someone who had finally hit some sort of an emotional wall. "Can you help us?"

"Already did help you," came the voice.

"I'm very thirsty from the hike. Do you have any water?" asked Ginny.

Although I'd brought some water along for both of us, the day was warm enough that, in retrospect, it wasn't nearly enough.

There was another pause from inside the shack. Then the gritty voice came again, sounding a little less forceful and more difficult to make out. "Go away."

"Please," said Ginny firmly. "You know you want to help."

It was almost as if Ginny needed her faith in humanity restored. She needed to find a good person after having seen infection destroy humanity and seeing the worst side of humanity when she'd been hijacked.

Finally, the door to the shack was pushed open. Ginny walked right in and I followed with more temerity. But when my eyes had adjusted to the darkness of the home, I relaxed. The shooter was an old, frail man with a bald head and an old plaid shirt and khakis. Then I frowned. He was very elderly, yes. Maybe he wasn't quite as frail as he appeared at first glance. He was wiry, actually.

"I'll get you water," he said abruptly. He strode away from us and returned with two clean glasses full of water. He'd even put a cube of ice in both glasses.

Ginny talked about Ty to the man. He listened with a stoic expression on his face. At the end of her story he said again, "I haven't seen him." But this time he added, "I'm sorry."

I was glad that Ginny hadn't asked for any food because I had the strong suspicion that there probably was hardly any in the house. I didn't think that this man stocked much food even *before* the crisis and he certainly hadn't popped out to the grocery store since.

I hesitated. Then I told myself that this man *had* saved our lives. I cleared my throat. "Ginny and I are going to head out to a retirement home where her grandmother lives. Her brother might be meeting her there. I don't know … that is … would you like to join us? I'm heading on after that, but it seems as if a retirement home might be a good place to hole up." I stopped speaking abruptly, feeling as though I was starting to ramble.

He was already shaking his head. "Not going to leave. This is where I was born and raised."

I said, "But it's not very safe here, clearly. And you probably don't have enough food or water to survive for long."

His eyes were blank and he shrugged a thin shoulder. "When it's time, it's time."

A shiver went up my spine. It sounded as if he was planning on suicide. I was about to insist that he follow me out to the retirement home before stopping. It was none of my business. This was obviously a special place to him, despite the condition of the shack. If he didn't want to leave it, that was something I should respect.

So instead, I just nodded. The old man regarded Ginny for a few moments, a sadness in his eyes. Finally he said gruffly, "I hope you find your brother. I hope he's okay. Don't give up hope."

Ginny nodded. She walked out of the shack, after carefully looking around through the dark to make sure the coast was clear.

As I was about to follow, the old man looked away and said, "The thing out there. Find supplies. Find a safe place. That thing I shot. It used to be my wife."

There was nothing I could say. I reached out and hugged him. And for a second, he clung to me.

Chapter Twenty

Ty

I watched as Charlie jogged up to the zombie family's house. It felt creepy looking at it. You could tell it had been a nice family at one point—they had kids' toys outside and a sandbox and even a garden with vegetables growing. It was so weird to realize that they probably just were hanging around outside, maybe watering their tomatoes or watching their kids bike around when they were infected.

My family, on the other hand, had *never* really been like one of those wholesome family sitcoms. Mom and Dad were *fine*, but they weren't all that involved with Ginny and me. We didn't have a lot of time together as a family with both of them working … and because Mom and Dad just liked it that way. For the first time since this whole thing started, I felt sad, actually sad. Here was this nice, normal looking family and it got infected like this. Now the family was running around trying to infect other people. What a waste.

Some movement out of the corner of my eye got my attention. I turned quickly in time to see the zombie family shambling in the direction of their old home. Did they have some fraction of memory left from before? Or were they just attracted to Charlie?

Mojo started a low growl.

I snapped to finally. They were definitely heading for Charlie. And when he put that garage door up, they might go right inside, which would mess up any plans Charlie might have for getting back in there.

I put my fingers in my mouth and gave a piercing whistle. Sure enough, the zombies spun around and started weaving in my direction. Mojo snarled and barked and appeared ready to run for the house, which he knew Charlie had entered.

This time I whistled to Mojo, who reluctantly followed me as I moved along the edge of the woods. The last thing I wanted was to lose Mojo. Right now, and after all I'd been through in the last few days, that might be the last straw.

The zombie family stumbled after us as I led them away. We were now fairly far away from the house. Mojo gave me an anxious look. He wasn't happy being so far away from Charlie.

I have to admit I was pretty relieved when I heard the welcome sound of a car engine revving. When I turned my head, I saw it was an older model Ford pickup truck. The zombies turned toward the sound of the engine, but their faces stayed blank, not recognizing the vehicle as something that had once belonged to them.

I whistled once more to Mojo and we started running in the direction of the truck. The zombies couldn't keep up and we easily lost them. Charlie stopped and pushed open the truck's passenger door and Mojo and I leaped in.

"Are you okay?" asked Charlie, looking at both of us with open concern. "That took me a while. The keys ended up being on the floor under the husband's jeans in the closet. Their house was pretty tidy except for that one pile. The keys I had didn't fit the truck."

"It was fine. You know how slow these zombies are. Mojo and I could have run circles around them," I said. But I was panting just the same, and so was Mojo.

"Okay. So we've got the truck. Let's head back on the road and get as close to our stuff as we can. We'll grab it just to keep it safe since it's so valuable now. Then I'll follow you on the bike to the retirement community," said Charlie.

We set out on the road, trying to get as close as possible to the point in the woods where the equipment was. I felt a lot better about life from the seat of the truck. It was amazing how you didn't feel as exposed when you were sitting up high in a truck.

Charlie, who seemed like a really laid back kind of guy, was pretty tensed up until the point when we got back to the stuff and he saw it was still there. I guess once he'd had his stuff stolen, he was always going to think it could happen again. I helped him load everything in the back of the truck. Then Charlie drove to where he'd left the motorcycle, climbed out of the truck, and hopped on.

"Why don't you keep Mojo in the truck with you?" he asked. "He's bound to be more comfortable that way."

I nodded. I was still trying to make sure I knew how to drive the truck since it was very different from the van. Actually, since I'd *only* driven the van, driving anything else was going to be a learning curve.

Charlie looked like he picked up on this. "Hey, you know where all the stuff is on the truck? Can you drive it?" His forehead wrinkled.

"No problem," I said. At least I knew where the accelerator and brakes were. Luckily, it was an automatic. Anything else I could figure out later.

We set out down the road with me leading. I wasn't going very fast, considering I wasn't used to driving the truck. The whole time we were leaving the area, I had my eyes peeled for Ginny. I still felt really guilty leaving the woods. I could only hope that somehow she'd taken the van to see Nana. I didn't want to think about what might have happened to her otherwise.

The retirement home was, as I'd told Charlie, kind of in the middle of nowhere. But there was a small town that I'd forgotten about along the way. It was the kind of small town that wouldn't leave much of an impression on you if you were driving through on your way to someplace else.

Charlie motioned at me to pull over and talk. I put the window of the truck down to listen to him and Mojo jumped on my lap and stuck his head out of the window to stare at Charlie with a big dog grin on his face.

"Do you know anything about this town?" asked Charlie. "It looks really small, and right now, kind of deserted."

I thought about it for a second. "I want to say that my dad mentioned that this town used to have a lot of people living here when he was a kid. They worked at a nearby mill. But then the mill closed down and years later a lot of the people in the town moved away. So yeah—it's pretty deserted, I think. All the time."

Charlie nodded, looking toward the small downtown. "Makes sense. I was just thinking that it might be a good idea to shore up our supplies. If it was easy and pretty safe and if we're not taking something that might belong to somebody else."

Especially since I was making a big dent in the supplies now. My mom always used to say that I ate her out of house and home. Teen boys are known for that. I wasn't feeling real excited about taking supplies since the last time I'd done it I'd run into trouble. But Charlie was right. The supplies were only going to last for so long. And I wasn't sure what the situation at the retirement home was. Maybe it was full of zombies. We should take this opportunity while we could.

"Sure," I said, taking a deep breath. "Let's check out the town."

Charlie drove to a side street and parked the bike next to the building. I pulled in next to him.

We glanced around us for a few minutes. Then he said, "We probably need to always assume that there are zombies around. And even though we don't see any people, we need to assume they're here too, holed up maybe. I don't want to break into any homes with people in them, so maybe we should knock on the door first." He grinned. "Although that seems very polite under the circumstances. It's just that I don't want to destroy the windows or doors on somebody's safe house."

I nodded, feeling relieved. That was something I was worried about too. It was good that Charlie and I were on the same page.

So that's what we did. We tried to be quiet, too, just in case there were any zombies to attract. The first place we saw was a diner right in the middle of the downtown. No one answered the knock and Mojo didn't act like he heard anything, so Charlie knocked again—firm but not too loud. When there was still no sign of anyone, Charlie took his elbow and broke the glass in the front door. He reached in and turned the lock.

I decided that Charlie hadn't always been a medic.

The diner was dark, so we hit the light switch. Nothing happened. Charlie cursed. "Looks like we're already having some pockets of power outages. Let's hope it comes back on and that it's not too widespread. I'm not ready for the power to be out for good yet."

The deserted diner gave me the creeps and I reached down and rubbed Mojo, the feel of the big dog relaxing me a little. I whispered, "Why don't you take the kitchen and I'll see if there's anything in the storeroom to take. And I'll look for big bags or boxes, too." I just wanted to get out of there as fast as we could.

I found a box in the storeroom that was almost empty. I dumped the contents out on the floor and then started loading it up with soft drinks, hamburger and hot dog buns, chips—just whatever I could find to throw in there.

"We'll have a cookout tonight, Ty!" said Charlie with a whoop. "Some good stuff left here."

"Great," I said, but I know I sounded less than enthusiastic. I was getting a bad feeling about this place. I glanced at Mojo, who trotted through the storeroom door. He looked relaxed and happy with his tongue lolling out. Maybe he was already picturing the feast he was going to have later on. I felt better seeing that the dog was so laid back.

"Did you find any boxes?" asked Charlie.

I grabbed one that was partially full of paper products, dumped it out and walked into the kitchen. Charlie was in the diner's fridge and pulled stuff out as fast as he could. I slid the box next to him and he started flinging things in.

We both froze when the bell on the front door of the diner rang. Charlie cursed. "I should have locked it behind us, deserted or not."

Mojo was no longer relaxed. The fur on the back of his neck rose up. Charlie motioned for me to hide in the janitor closet. I shook my head and opened a drawer. I pulled out a knife. Charlie frowned at me but also reached in the drawer for a knife.

Charlie told Mojo to stay. The dog was about as obedient as I was. At least he waited until Charlie had stealthily walked out the door before he slunk along after him.

We heard a chair knock over in the main room and Charlie and I glanced at each other. That wasn't a good sign. Zombies were clumsy. We crept closer to the sounds we were hearing.

We'd apparently left the lights in the on position because suddenly there was a power surge and the lights flickered on and off again. Finally they stayed on. We saw a figure weaving around the center of the room. It stumbled against a chair, knocking it to the side.

"Do you think there's a back door?" I muttered to Charlie, my voice shaking. Because even though we had knives, I didn't really like my chances with a knife against a zombie. I didn't want to get that close.

Then the figure turned, and Charlie said under his breath, "I don't think that's a zombie."

Chapter Twenty-One

Charlie

The figure in front of us wasn't a zombie but a middle-aged man wearing a button-down shirt and khaki pants. His clothes were stained and wrinkled. His eyes were bloodshot and glassy but not empty like the zombies' eyes were. And his mouth wasn't as slack as the zombies' were, either. But he was stumbling around just like he was infected. Then I figured it out.

"Drunk as a skunk," I murmured to Ty.

The man didn't seem especially worried about Ty and me, despite the knives we were holding. He gazed at us and then said in a thick and slurring voice, "Thanks for getting me in here, guys. I'm Trent."

I lowered his knife. "No problem. Looking for something, are you?"

Trent shrugged and seemed to concentrate very hard on sitting down. "About to run out of booze. Can't face the end of the world sober, you know."

I sat down near Trent but Ty wasn't as excited about hanging out with him. Instead, he walked over to the front door and locked it as best he could. At least a zombie wouldn't be able to figure out how to make it through. I'd been so intent on our quick foray that I couldn't believe I'd been sloppy about locking the door. And it would have been nice to have brought a gun inside, too. Next time I wouldn't be so slack.

I said, "Who else is left in this town? Have you been able to get out and assess the situation?"

This man looked like he wasn't really able to even assess his own situation. He said, "Nobody here."

Ty gave a shiver and I couldn't help but agree with him. The idea of this being some sort of little ghost town was pretty creepy.

"Nobody at all?" asked Ty. "Are you sure?"

The man turned in his chair to look at Ty and nearly fell out of it. "Nobody *alive*. Just those infected dead people."

"Why haven't you left?" Ty still lingered near the door.

The man shrugged again. "No point. I'd have to keep running. If there are zombies here in this town, there are zombies in *all* the towns. That means I'd have to keep going from place to place to find supplies and escape infected people." He stopped talking, shaking his head. Then he put a hand to his forehead like it hurt.

I said in my most authoritative voice, "There's a better plan. You could come with us."

The man looked at me unsteadily and then gave a short laugh. "Right. Because you're *not* running."

"I'm getting Ty connected with family in a retirement community. That might be a good option since they would have food and rooms and living areas. Then I'm going to head out into the woods or another rural area and set up there. I can do some small-scale farming and hunting. You can come along."

The man gave me a scornful look. "And that's a life?"

I frowned at him. "Better than getting drunk and

waiting to be infected."

"Says who?" Trent's eyes were suddenly exhausted. "What have I got to live for? My family has been infected. I'm guessing that my friends are, too. My life wasn't even all that great before this happened, and it sure hasn't gotten better now."

Usually, I was a pretty chilled out guy. Everyone always said how laid back I was. But this guy's hopelessness really got to me. He'd basically just thrown in the towel and given up—on the very first week of the zombie apocalypse. And, for whatever reason, there was just something in my genetic makeup that couldn't leave this alone.

"Look, it's way too early in this crisis to just give up hope," I said briskly. "Join up with Ty and me."

But my persuasive speech was cut off. Ty leapt back away from the door when suddenly there were loud thumps and knocks at the other side, along with a rattling of the doorknob. Mojo whined, ears back, tail down.

"Zombies," said Ty. "They won't be able to figure out how to get around the locked door."

"Unless they just break the thing down," muttered Trent.

"Let me in!" demanded a frantic woman's voice.

I ran to the door.

"I wouldn't open it," said Trent laconically. "Sounds like those things are chasing her."

I shot him a look through narrowed eyes and yanked the door open, pulling the woman, a frail brunette, inside as fast as I could. But before I could force the door shut, several zombies pushed their way in, grabbing at me. I reared back and lifted my leg up to kick one of them in the stomach as hard as I could, but it somehow managed to get my leg.

I struggled hard to get away, sweat pouring out of me, hopping on one leg and trying desperately to get away. Until Mojo flung himself at the zombie, knocking it backward across the floor.

"Run!" yelled Ty. "Come on, out the back!"

The woman was already ahead of us, running for the back door. Ty was following her. "I'll grab the stuff, Charlie," he called to me.

Trent sat calmly at the table as if there weren't predators in the room with him.

"Trent!" I barked. "Come on!"

Trent sat still, gazing wearily at me as the zombies stumbled closer to him. "You know you can't take that woman with you. She was bitten on the arm. I saw it."

I shook my head at him in frustration. "Trent! Let's go!"

"Get out of here," he said with a sigh, picking up his glass and draining it with one gulp as a zombie reached for him.

I heard Ty's voice, frightened but strong at the same time. "Charlie?"

"On my way," I said, running now, as a zombie in a suit and tie shambled toward me.

I ran through the kitchen and grabbed one of the boxes that Ty was struggling with. "Okay," I said, "let's get out of here."

We didn't have much time since there was already a zombie, who apparently used to be someone's grandmother, heading in our direction. Fortunately, I felt pretty good about my chances avoiding this particular zombie. But there were sure to be others right behind her.

Ty whispered urgently to me as we jogged to the back door with the supplies, "So what are we doing about the woman? Trent said she was infected."

I felt a pang just thinking about Trent and how I'd left him to his fate. "Trent wasn't exactly thinking straight, was he?" I muttered to Ty.

"Yeah, but what if he's right? Should we take her along? They turn pretty fast sometimes," said Ty in a low voice.

Sure enough, as we headed out the back, the woman was bent over, clutching her stomach and moaning. It wasn't a good sign.

Suddenly, I realized the danger I'd been willing to put Ty in, all because of my desire to save the world. Whatever superhero complex I had, it needed to stop. Because I'd have pulled out with Mojo on the bike and left Ty to his fate with the infected woman in the truck. I hadn't thought it through.

Ashamed of myself, I shifted the box and put a hand on Ty's back. "I'm sorry, man. You're absolutely right. We've got to leave her behind. She must have been infected, just like Trent said."

We threw the boxes in the back of the truck.

"How do we get rid of her?" asked Ty uneasily. "She's probably not going to want to stay."

Most likely not. Especially since she'd just been shrieking and running in terror away from the zombies. I couldn't see her volunteering to hang out at Zombie Diner.

Almost as if she could read my thoughts, the woman, sweating profusely, straightened up and grabbed the passenger door to the truck, climbing inside.

I groaned. It had been a rough week. I'd gone from sitting in an ambulance intent on saving lives, to allowing someone I could have saved to die. And now it looked as if I was going to throw someone to the wolves. Practically literally.

I squared my shoulders and quickly grabbed the door handle of the truck to open it and pull out the woman. Despite her obvious illness, she saw what I was doing and locked the doors to the truck.

I swore under my breath. "Ty? The keys?"

Ty handed them over to me. "Charlie? The zombies are on their way out." His voice was urgent.

I swore again. "Ty, hop on the bike with Mojo and get away."

Ty shook his head, looking frantic. "Charlie, I don't know how to even start the bike."

Sometimes I forgot he was only fifteen. "It's okay," I said in as calm and steady a voice as I could muster. "We're gonna get out of here. You and Mojo get ready to hop in the front seat, okay? But not until I pull her out of the truck, just in case she's already turned."

Ty moved around to the driver's side and Mojo followed him as he whistled softly to the dog.

I jammed the key into the lock and then held on the door. Despite pulling on the door with all her strength, the woman was no match for me, especially as sick as she was.

Then I saw it, right as I had the door fully open. Her eyes went blank, her mouth went slack. And she started moaning. She reached for me.

I unceremoniously grabbed her by the legs and jerked her out of the truck. I pushed the lock in, slammed the door, handed off the keys to Ty, and then scrambled to the bike before she could get back up. Or before more zombies could find their way outside.

We drove for miles before Ty motioned to me to pull over. "Hey," he said, and his eyes were exhausted, "let's not stop again. I don't think I can handle any more excitement right now. I just want to get to a safe place and rest a little."

"No more stops," I promised him. "Straight to your Nana."

Admittedly, I hadn't spent much time hanging out at retirement homes in the past. But there had been a few visits when I was a teen and my mom took me to see my great-aunt. I remember that they were bustling places. There were residents boarding vans for various excursions, taking strolls, and participating in lots of scheduled activities.

It was eerie to pull up to the Crofton Retirement Community and see the wrought-iron gates shut. It was even eerier to see no sign of life on the grounds of the community.

Ty pulled up beside me and rolled the window of the truck down. Mojo scooted over to stick his head out the window and grin at me.

"Okay," I said to Ty, "so what's the best way to get in this place?"

Ty's face was drawn with exhaustion and worry and I could tell he didn't have his A-game on. The sun was low in the sky. He was clearly getting overwhelmed. "When everything was normal, there'd either be some guy working the gate, or else we'd intercom in and someone would open it up."

It *was* a gated community. But it was the kind of gate that wasn't going to keep zombies out. It was just going to keep our vehicles out unless we got them to open up. And right now, I didn't fancy the proposition of abandoning the truck and walking through the grounds exposed.

I especially didn't fancy it when I looked through the gate and saw a white-haired gentleman in navy pajamas who was staggering up to the gate, gazing hungrily at us.

Mojo growled and shifted on the seat.

Ty gave a shaky sigh.

"Hey man, just because we see one infected resident here doesn't mean they're all that way," I said with a confidence I didn't really feel.

Ty said in a low voice, "If I see Nana wandering up to me, I think I'm going to be sick."

"We're thinking positive, right? Actually, let's see if we can think better right now than we have been. We have a problem. We need to get through these gates and drive right up to the door so we don't have to encounter Zombie Zeke over there. So how are we going to do it?" I asked. I was asking myself as much as asking Ty.

"Can you try the buzzer again?"

I did. And again. We waited for a minute and listened to see if a voice would come through the speaker or if the gate would suddenly lift up. Neither happened.

"Ty, I'm thinking we need to honk the horn. Alert someone in there that we're out here."

Ty scanned the grounds. "Won't that bring more zombies out? What if the reason we're not getting any answer is because they're *all* zombies in there?"

I spoke calmly since I was worried that Ty was getting worked up over his grandmother. "Then why are we only seeing Zombie Zeke? How many people live here at Crofton?"

Ty shrugged a shoulder. "I don't know. It's a pretty big place. Maybe a hundred people? Something like that?"

"So why aren't we seeing all the MeMaws and PawPaws out wandering around the grounds? No, I think there are some uninfected people in there. Let's take the risk. Honk the truck's horn and maybe we'll catch their attention. Then I can hit the buzzer some more and I bet you that somebody will answer us," I said.

Ty took in a deep breath. Staring at Zombie Zeke, he gave a few taps of the horn. It wasn't as loud or as long as I wanted, but I pressed the buzzer again. And again.

Nothing.

Ty lay on the horn this time. It was a long, insistent blast. And the truck was a deep, serious-sounding base. Then he paled a little, motioning at the grounds.

A good fifty or more elderly residents flooded onto the grounds toward us. They were on the grass, which was still carefully manicured. They were stomping through the carefully tended flower beds. And they were streaming down the road leading to the gate.

I cursed, softly.

Chapter Twenty-Two

Mallory

By the time we got back to the car, it was pitch black. It was lucky I'd thought to carry flashlights with us, or we'd never have been able to find our way back.

"Let's just sleep in the car tonight and then head out early to see your Nana," I said. "It will be easier to see what the situation is like at the retirement home when the sun is up and we can see."

Then I was kicking myself because a worried line appeared on Ginny's brow. "You think maybe those things are in the retirement home?"

"No, I don't think that. I like to stay positive. But I do want to be able to make absolutely sure the coast is clear when we get there. It's good to think positively, but it's good to be safe, too."

Ginny relaxed a little. "That sounds good." She yawned. "I'm pretty tired, anyway. Do you think we'll be safe when we sleep?"

I wasn't sure which was more dangerous—the zombies that were rapidly spreading the virus, or the dangerous, uninfected people like the ones Ginny had run into. I had a feeling that parking on the side of the road wasn't a great idea.

"I'm going to drive on a little ways and see if I can find a good spot to park the car where we might be hidden. Do you know much about the route to the retirement home? Are there any towns you go through, anything like that?" I asked.

Ginny frowned in concentration. "There's one small town that sometimes we stop in for gas on the way. I've gotten an ice cream there before, too."

"But we haven't passed it?"

Ginny shook her head.

"Okay. Let's drive on for a while and see if we can get to the town. If not, I'll find a spot in the woods to park. Maybe a driveway, or something that's off the main road," I said.

Ginny nodded, but looked worried. The fact she'd been hijacked last time was clearly on her mind.

I kept driving in the fading light. For a while, all we passed was a heavily forested area full of pine trees. But after a while, I noticed signs pointing us to the small town of Emerson.

Emerson was one of those small towns that had probably allowed itself to fall into disrepair at some pint, but was now trying harder. Old brick buildings in its downtown now housed what appeared to be galleries, shops, and a diner. The awnings and signs over the businesses were new and cheerful.

Ginny stared out the window, as if longing for a glimpse of something stable and normal. But there was no sign of life. Or of death.

"Can we just park the car and see if we can stay in one of these shops or something?" asked Ginny. Maybe they have fresher food there. And the floor might be more comfortable than sleeping in the car.

Part of me wanted to agree with her. The only problem was that we had no idea what the situation was like in the town of Emerson. For all we knew, there could be zombies roaming the streets at night. And it was night now.

So I reluctantly said, "Better not, sweetie. I think we're safer in the car. We'll just keep the doors locked, keep the car hidden, and we'll be fine."

I drove a little while to see if there was a good place to park the car for the night. Finally I found the gas station that Ginny had mentioned. I shivered, thinking of what had happened to Joshua at a gas station. I pushed those memories firmly aside. "There's a car wash there. That might be a good place to hide."

"*Inside* the car wash?" A faint hint of a smile from Ginny now. "I always love the car wash. Especially the kinds that have the things that come down and wipe the car off."

"I like those, too. But I'm thinking we should maybe park just on the other side of the car wash. Out of sight." But not inside where we could be trapped by zombies. A fact I didn't want to mention to Ginny.

After we'd parked and turned off the engine, Ginny put her seat all the way back and quickly fell asleep. It took me a while longer. I kept thinking I was seeing movement in the nearby woods. Finally, I fell into a fitful sleep.

Hours later I woke up, feeling I was being stared at. I turned my stiff neck slowly to the left and froze as I saw a teenage girl with a long ponytail staring at me with blank eyes and her mouth agape. Her mangled body told her story. She lifted a hand and pressed it against the car window, growling at me.

I didn't make a sound, not wanting to scare Ginny who was still soundly sleeping beside me. But I quickly started the car and firmly stepped on the accelerator, leaving the teen zombie staggering slowly after us.

Ginny had given me enough of an idea of the direction of her grandmother's retirement home that I felt confident enough to head off without consulting her. I'd slept longer than I'd planned on, anyway. It was dawn now and getting lighter every minute. With darkness no longer lending us its cover, I was ready to keep moving.

As we sped down the road, I experienced a mix of feelings. For one, I knew that connecting Ginny with the family she had left was the best thing for her. But I also realized that I felt sorry for myself. I'd wanted children for so long—it had been the reason that I'd run into problems with my boyfriend. And now, with Ginny beside me, I almost felt like a mother. It would be hard on me to let her go.

I drove for what felt like a long while and then saw a small sign off to the right as I went past. I stopped and backed up the car to read it. The sign pointed to a small entrance for Crofton Retirement Home. I turned down the road and stopped, realizing that it was a gated community ... and the wrought-iron gate was closed. The gatehouse wasn't occupied, but I saw a speaker and a call button.

I rolled the window down but decided that before I pressed the button, I should make sure it was the right place. "Ginny," I said, "We're here. I think. Is this the right place?"

She lifted her head sleepily to look around. When she spotted the gatehouse she smiled. "This is it!"

I hit the buzzer. And waited. No answer from the speaker on the gate.

"Is this usually the way you get inside?" I asked.

"No, there's always a guy who lets us in," said Ginny, rubbing the sleep out of her eyes and squinting to see better. "Is there a sign or something that tells us what to do if no one's here?"

I pushed the button again and said, "No, I think we're just supposed to hit this buzzer."

I pushed the button repeatedly for the next ten minutes. I was about ready to just abandon the car and walk with Ginny through the wooded grounds when a woman's voice finally spoke. "Who's there?" she asked. Her voice was strained and breathless as if she'd just finished running.

A relieved smile played around Ginny's lips, but I didn't share her relief. Not yet. Something seemed off here.

"My name is Mallory and I'm traveling with a young girl named Ginny whose grandmother is a resident here. Could you let us in there?"

There was a long, empty pause. I swear I could still hear the nurse breathing heavily.

Ginny said in a loud voice that could carry to the speaker, "Please? Please let us in. I'm also looking for my brother, Ty. He was taking care of me. He's fifteen. Is he here?" She leaned forward eagerly, eyes trained on the intercom on the gate.

Another very long pause. Then the woman's voice said slowly, "I'm not sure you really want to come in here. It's not safe. There are undead here."

Ginny made a strangled noise. I was getting tired of the stalling and said briskly, "Open the gate. We'll decide for ourselves how long we want to stay, but we need to come in and assess the situation here."

Another pause. Then, finally, the gate was opened.

"Okay, so we'll keep the doors locked. Let's be super-careful when we get out of the car and go in the main door. That woman wasn't very helpful, wasn't she?" I muttered.

Ginny's hand clutched the door handle so hard her knuckles were white.

The driveway to the retirement home was long and winding. I caught my breath when I spotted movement out of the corner of my eye and turned in time to see an elderly woman in a long nightgown wandering like a ghost through the trees in the early morning light. She turned as we approached and snarled at me. I shivered and glanced at Ginny. I was relieved to see she was staring out her own window and hadn't seen the figure.

I wouldn't have chosen to come here with Ginny, but I knew she couldn't rest until she'd searched for her family. For me, I just wanted to keep traveling, hopefully with Ginny, to the safe house.

I found a parking spot in a very empty lot next to the building. Ginny said, "A lot of the people at Crofton don't drive anymore."

I was just glad I wasn't trying to hijack a car. There was really nothing here to choose from. And nothing looked abandoned.

"Ready?" I asked Ginny, my hand on the car door.

She nodded, taking in a deep breath. We opened our doors and stepped out, hurrying to the glass doors of the retirement home.

As we stepped in the expansive entranceway, I gasped. There was a group of what had been residents in the sitting area inside. They were leaning on walkers and sitting in wheelchairs and staring blankly at us, moaning. They moved toward us.

Ginny looked frozen beside me. "Ginny, lead the way," I said sharply. "To your Nana's room. Come on. They'll move slowly."

And they certainly did. They hadn't even moved a

few feet by the time Ginny and I had run out of the room and to an elevator.

She pushed the elevator button and looked worriedly behind us as we waited for the elevator to come down. "Are they coming?" she whispered.

"Not yet." I paused. "Do you know how to get to your grandmother's room?"

"Sort of," said Ginny. "I know what floor and what hall she's on. The only problem is that all the rooms look alike. But she has a table outside her room with a vase and a bouquet of fake flowers on it. So we can find it as long as she hasn't changed it."

The elevator finally arrived on our floor with a dinging sound. The doors opened and we jumped back as we spotted an elderly man wearing navy pants and a checkered button-down shirt who looked very ill. I noticed he had a nasty cut on his neck.

"He's just been infected," I murmured to Ginny. "Is there another elevator?"

Just behind us, the crowd from the sitting room finally caught up with us.

"I don't know if there's another elevator or not," said Ginny in a rush, staring at the residents staggering and wheeling toward us.

"We'll find out," I said, grabbing her arm and taking off down a long hall. "If nothing else, we'll take the stairs."

On the other end of the building, through a couple of sitting areas with various zombie nurses and zombie residents snarling at us as we went, we finally found another elevator. We carefully checked inside this time before boarding it, and were relieved to find there was no one in there.

"Fourth floor," mumbled Ginny, hitting the button.

We didn't say a word on the short ride up. I think

we were steeling ourselves for what we might find on the fourth floor.

When the elevator door swung open, we cautiously peered down the hall. The lights flickered on and off. The electrical grid must be wavering. I remembered that it was dependent on people to run it—and if people were running for their lives, the chances were that we wouldn't have power for much longer.

As if reading my mind, the lights went out. But there was a glowing strip along the bottom of the wall that must run on a generator as a safety precaution for when the power went out at the Home. It was down this dimly lit hallway that Ginny and I walked. She turned her head swiftly from side to side as she tried to figure out where she was in the hallway.

About three-quarters of the way down the hallway, Ginny stopped short. "Here it is," she said with relief. "The table with the flowers on it."

There was also a decorative plaque on the door with a rainbow and a mountain scene on it. Ginny knocked on the door. There was no answer. Ginny knocked again and a small voice from inside said, "Who's there?"

"It's me, Nana. It's Ginny."

The door slowly opened a crack and an old woman with wild hair peered suspiciously out. She stared at Ginny wordlessly for a moment as if shocked to see her there. And Ginny, relieved to see her and also desperate to get out of the dark hall, nearly knocked the woman down with the enthusiasm of her hug.

Now the woman opened the door wide and I followed Ginny farther in. I closed the door behind us, locking it securely.

The room was about as untidy as Ginny's Nana, but I supposed that's to be expected during what appeared to be the end of civilization as we knew it.

Ginny was bubbly with a mixture of relief and anxiety. "Nana, I'm so glad to see you. I was worried about you."

The old woman beamed at her with bright blue eyes. "Oh, you shouldn't worry about me. Everything is all right."

I reached out a hand to the old lady. "I'm Mallory."

She reached out her own hand. "Clarice Brown."

"Have you seen Ty, Nana? He got me out of town, but then we got separated. He and I were trying to get here to find you," said Ginny quickly.

Ginny's Nana frowned in concentration.

"Have you seen Ty?" repeated Ginny. "Is he here?"

There was a short pause and then Ginny's Nana said, "Who's Ty?"

Chapter Twenty-Three

Ty

Even though it looked like the whole retirement home had turned into zombies and were heading our way, I knew I couldn't leave until I'd found out if Nana and Ginny were here and what had happened to them. But I felt bad asking Charlie to be part of this. I didn't want to be alone and facing this stuff on my own, but it didn't feel right making Charlie risk his life to help me out. After all, it wasn't *his* sister or *his* grandmother.

"Listen," I said urgently to him, "you've done enough for me. You got me here safely and I appreciate it. But you and Mojo need to get out of here, now."

Charlie was still pressing the button on the gate. "Come on, come on," he muttered. He didn't look like he was listening to me at all.

"Seriously," I said, watching as the zombie old folks were heading slowly but surely toward us. "Get out of here. I can just run in and down the road to the retirement home."

Charlie turned to look at me in surprise. "What? Through a herd of zombies? You're not thinking this through."

"No, I'm totally thinking it through," I said. "I can run circles around young zombies and these are *old* zombies. I think the odds are in my favor, even if there are a lot of them."

Charlie shook his head and pressed the button again. "No, man. Not with gobs of them like that. There might be zombies lining the drive all the way to the front entrance of the Home. You're a great runner, don't get me wrong, but there's only so far you can run without resting."

He looked in frustration at the speaker again and banged it with his fist. Finally, a woman's voice spoke. "Who's there?" it asked suspiciously.

Charlie shot me a relieved look and then said quickly, "I'm Charlie. I'm outside your gate with a teen named Ty whose grandmother is one of your residents."

No word from the speaker.

"We need to get inside the gates," said Charlie impatiently. He rolled his eyes at me.

Silence from the speaker.

I spoke up this time, trying to make my voice sound younger and innocent and scared. It wasn't hard to do, considering the circumstances. "Ma'am?" I asked. "He's telling the truth. My name is Ty and I'm looking for my grandmother, who lives here. I'm also looking for my younger sister, Ginny, who might have come here separately, looking for my Nana."

Finally the voice spoke again. "What's your Nana's name?" She still sounded real suspicious.

I cleared my throat and said, "Clarice Brown."

There was silence from the speaker again.

I felt anxiety mounting again. "Did you hear me? Clarice Brown. She's a resident here. She's lived here for the last seven years."

Charlie swore softly under his breath, clearly frustrated. "Look, are you a nurse or a staff member or what? We need to come in. We've got a crowd of zombies heading our way and the relative of a resident who needs admittance."

The voice now sounded crafty. "Sounds like you're in a bad way. But if I help you out, how can you help *me* out?"

Charlie shot me a disbelieving look. "Are you kidding me?" he demanded of the speaker. In a furious whisper he said to me, "Ty, are you sure we need to go in there? There's something wrong. I mean, something *badly* wrong in there."

I nodded silently.

Charlie sighed and pushed his lips together tightly, staring at the invading horde of elderly zombies heading slowly but surely our way. "What is it that you need? We have some provisions with us. But you've surely got a lot more over in the kitchen there. What you probably *don't* have over there is a couple of young, healthy men to carry or load things. I'm thinking you need us a lot more than we need you."

Another thoughtful pause on the other end. The voice was low enough for us to have to strain to hear it. "But I have the young man's Nana. And maybe some information about his little sister. But there is something that I need. If I let you in the gates, you will promise to deliver what I ask."

Charlie waved his hands in the air helplessly. "I don't think we really have a choice, Ty. I'd have gladly helped them out *anyway*, if they'd needed it ... before she started pressuring us. Now I've *got* to help, but I'm not happy about it."

I nodded again. Mojo stiffened at the frustrated tone in his master's voice and I gave him a rub. Charlie was one of those people who really lived to serve. I remember how he was so determined to help even the drunk guy at the diner who didn't want to live.

"All right. We're coming in. We'll give you some help. Now open the gate," said Charlie.

Finally the wrought iron gate opened. The elderly zombies were about to reach us by now, so it was just in time. Charlie revved his bike engine and sped down the winding road leading to Crofton. I followed quickly. Mojo sat at attention in the passenger seat, looking out the window at the staggering infected residents dressed primarily in their nightclothes.

We pulled right up to the building in an almost empty parking lot. I remembered that most of the residents here no longer drove their cars, which would explain why there were hardly any here. I glanced around the parking lot and didn't see any zombies lingering around. "We should be able to make it in okay," I said in a low voice, making sure I didn't attract them by speaking too loud.

Charlie nodded and gave a low whistle to Mojo who joyfully jumped out of the truck. I smiled at the thought of the big dog trotting down the halls of the retirement community. What wouldn't have been imaginable a week ago was now the new normal. I saw that Charlie packed a small backpack with the gun and ammo.

The entrance hall right inside the front doors was usually full of people playing cards and watching visitors come and go. There was no one there now.

Charlie looked at all the empty seats and tables and murmured, "Is it usually this quiet here?"

I shook my head. "Think they're all locked up in their rooms, scared to come out?"

This was what I hoped was true and not that all the residents were now infected.

Charlie gave an uncertain shrug. "There were a

lot of zombies out there, don't get me wrong. But I'd like to think that there are still some residents here that haven't gotten sick."

"We should probably go to the front desk," I said. "That's where the woman who spoke to us at the gate would have been."

"Yeah, let's go find out what Little Miss Sunshine wanted," said Charlie gruffly.

He followed me through the entrance hall to an adjoining hallway that had a tall counter that was usually staffed by at least one person. Charlie and I glanced at each other when it was clear there was no one there.

"Hello? Hello?" I called out softly.

There was a supply closet right behind the desk and we watched as a tall, thin, grim woman with untidy graying hair pulled into a bun stuck her head around the side of the door.

"We're your crew," said Charlie, still barely containing his irritation. "What do you know about Ty's grandmother and sister?"

The woman's mouth was pursed as if she were trying to decide how much information to feed us before we'd done anything to help her. She finally reluctantly said, "Clarice Brown is in her room." She hesitated as if there was more to say before firmly pressing her lips together. She gave Mojo a disapproving glare.

My heart gave a happy leap at the good news. "And my sister?" I asked. "Have you seen my sister here?"

Charlie looked at me with concern. I knew that he thought all along that Ginny hadn't made it out of the woods, but that he was too nice to say it.

The woman came around the side of the door.

"She did come through here. With a woman."

I shook my head, confused. "What woman? My mother is infected."

"It was a young woman in her twenties. They seemed to be friends," said the woman. She gave us a sly look. "And your sister left a note for you."

"She did? Where?" I felt that rush of happiness again. That feeling that things were going to work out after all.

Now the woman shook her head. "I'm not going to give you more information until you complete these tasks for me." Her blue eyes were hard as granite as she stared at us.

"First we're checking in with Ty's Nana," said Charlie, jabbing a finger at the desk to make his point. "Just to make sure you're not just feeding us some line you've made up to get us to run whatever errands you need."

The tall woman flashed an irritated glance at him. "I'm not lying to you."

"Fine. But you don't exactly seem trustworthy to me," said Charlie.

"I'm just trying not to give you too much information up front. We probably don't have much time to stand around and chat before those things catch up with us," said the woman impatiently. "And I assure you that I'm trustworthy. I'm a nurse here at Crofton."

"Which doesn't necessarily mean that you're trustworthy," said Charlie. "But go ahead and tell us what you want. After we've checked on Nana, we'll do our best to deliver it."

The woman came all the way away from the supply closet door to lean on the tall counter in front of us. In a raspy whisper she said, "I want you to get into the kitchen and get food out. The residents don't have any food to eat now and it's all in the kitchen area."

"And I'm assuming there is a reason that the kitchen isn't accessible to you," said Charlie smoothly. "Is it overrun with zombies?"

"Let's just say there are plenty in there," she said with a shrug of a thin shoulder.

"Is that it?" I asked. It didn't sound like much of a chore to me. After all, Charlie and I had both raided food pantries since the infection started.

"Not quite," she said. "We're also in need of medications. And the medical station area is full of those ... things."

"Here's my question," said Charlie, head tilted to the side. "You keep saying *we* and *the residents*. I don't hear any residents. The residents I see are already infected. So who is left and where are they? Corralled in their rooms?"

The nurse eyed him with dislike. She seemed like one of my old teachers: the kind of person who didn't want to be questioned. "The residents who aren't infected were at first in their separate rooms. Those rooms were scattered through the facility and accessing everyone without being subjected to an attack was impossible. We moved everyone into the memory care unit."

I said, "But the memory care unit is locked up from the *outside*. So the residents can't get *out*."

"And that helps, too. Because if the residents get out and go back to their rooms, I'm not going after them to feed them or give them medicine. I've also got the doors locked from the inside so that we can't be invaded by infected residents." The nurse's voice was totally calm as if she was talking about the flu.

Charlie gave a bob of his head. "Okay. So we get

as much food out as we can and then grab some medications from the infirmary. Got it. Although I do think your long-term plan sucks if it involves staying in the memory care unit with a little bit of stockpiled food."

"Your supplies won't last forever," I added. "Don't you think you should help get the residents out of Crofton?"

The nurse gave me a sort of sly smile. "Get your Nana out if you're determined to. But the rest of the residents and I are staying put. They were resigned to staying in the building even *before* this outbreak. I don't think they're feeling adventurous enough to leave during it."

She eyed Mojo again and her fingers restlessly pulled at her collar. "That dog shouldn't be in here, you know."

Charlie snorted. "Well, zombies shouldn't be in here either, but they are. If you want us, you get Mojo, too."

The nurse's face was as sour as if she had swallowed a lemon whole. I got the impression that she didn't want *any* of us, but that her options were real limited.

Then something occurred to me. "Hey, I remember security cameras in some of the common rooms."

Charlie held out his hand for a high-five. "Good thinking." He turned again to the nurse and snapped, "Don't you think that would have made our chances of succeeding just a little stronger?"

The nurse shrugged and directed us behind the desk. "Suit yourself." Her face was lined with unhappiness.

Charlie and I walked around the tall counter and

through a wooden door into a small room. There were monitors showing footage from different areas of Crofton.

Charlie and I looked at the cameras without talking for a few minutes. Then Charlie spoke to the nurse without even turning around. "Sending us on a suicide mission? Are you trying to get supplies or just trying to kill us?"

The infirmary and kitchen area were crawling with zombies.

Chapter Twenty-Four

Charlie

Looking at those monitors and seeing the zombies everywhere, I knew I didn't want Ty anywhere near it.

"Hey," I told him. "You stay here with Mojo. I've got this."

He shot me a disbelieving look. "Really? No way. Not with fifty of those things in the kitchen and another fifteen around the infirmary."

I tried making my voice light. "Yeah, but these zombies are like one hundred years old. They weren't in great shape even *before* they were infected. I'll just slip into the kitchen, fill up some boxes just like we did at the diner, and then take off. Then I'll go back and handle the infirmary." Even as I said it, though, I knew it sounded like a fairytale.

Ty knew it too. The kid wasn't stupid. "I'm going with you. Mojo can stay here. With both of us, it'll go a lot faster. I can distract the zombies while you grab the food. Then we can run out. I'll lure them into the dining room, since it'll be less cramped."

"No, *I'll* lure them and *you'll* get the stuff," I insisted. "Although I still wish you'd stay put."

Ty said quietly, "Maybe I was a kid a few days ago, but the last few days have made me grow up fast. You're not old, but I know one thing—I'm still a lot younger and faster than you are. I've got a better chance of making this work."

"Okay," I reluctantly agreed. Then I said, "Hey, why don't you see Nana real quick before we head over to the Zombie Lounge?"

Ty studied me out of slitted eyes. "Why? So that she can talk me out of going in there?"

Actually, yes. But I realized that Ty wasn't going to buy it. As I said before, he was a smart kid.

"Let's get this over with, then," I said grimly. I pulled off the small backpack that I'd grabbed that had the .22 and ammo. I hesitated and then asked Ty, "Do you know how to use this? Otherwise, I'll take it and try to provide you with cover."

"My dad was pretty anti-weapons," Ty said. "But I had a friend whose dad took us to the shooting range. He thought my dad knew. Plus I was in scouts, so I'm good with rifles, too."

I was satisfied enough to hand the gun over to him. In any other scenario, I couldn't picture myself giving a fifteen year old boy a gun. But other scenarios didn't include zombie infested retirement homes.

The grim nurse pointed us in the direction of the kitchen. "There should be some empty packing boxes in there that you can use to throw the food in," she said.

The wide halls lined with handrails were eerily silent as we walked down them. Mojo whined when I tried to make him stay, so I reluctantly allowed him to come with us. If we ran into trouble, we wouldn't have been able to return and get him anyway—it was better to have him with us.

Ty and I walked in silence, not wanting to attract any attention. Just the same, though, I still felt like we could be jumped on at any second from any of the adjoining rooms. It was a tense five minute walk to the dining room and kitchen.

We could hear the moaning sounds before we got to the dining room. Mojo's fur raised on his back and his eyes were steely. Whether it was true or not, Mojo seemed to think that he could take on zombies with no problem.

There was a hallway and a door that led to the kitchen. Ty and I listened outside the door for a few minutes to see if we could hear anything directly on the other side. Not hearing anything, I slowly pulled open the door and Ty aimed the gun inside the room. There was nothing there.

We moved quickly into the kitchen. Ty bobbed his head silently to me to indicate a stack of produce boxes that were wide and long enough to put a bunch of cans in.

We worked our way into the kitchen, pulling cans and other nonperishables off the shelves and putting them in the boxes. The boxes quickly grew very heavy, so we carried them out to the hallway when they were filled.

A warning growl from Mojo made us freeze. Sure enough, hovering in the doorway was a zombie employee moaning at us. I glanced at Ty. The original plan suddenly didn't seem like such a good idea. It would be tricky to squeeze past this guy and distract the rest of the zombies by luring them into the far side of the adjoining dining room. Besides, we'd already filled up six or seven flat boxes of supplies. I shook my head at Ty and pointed out the back of the kitchen, the way we'd come in. We had enough food for a while. Enough food to give the nurse what she wanted so that she'd tell Ty about his sister.

The zombie's wandering had somehow grabbed

the attention of the other zombies. Now there were others, some former residents and some former staff, that were pushing into the kitchen behind the first one, swinging their heads to look around.

"Let's get out of here," breathed Ty.

I agreed. I wasn't even exactly sure how we were going to lug all the food we'd already gotten. We exited the door we'd first entered, and Ty and I barricaded it with a heavy armchair from a nearby sitting room. We spotted an abandoned motorized wheelchair and Ty hopped in. I piled food into the basket on the front of the chair and stacked it on Ty's lap. I held the other boxes of food, my muscles straining with the weight.

Driving the chair seemed pretty easy, but it was pretty painfully slow. Ty kept stealing glances behind us. "Think they'll bust out of that door?" he asked as the chair, now really weighted down, crawled down the hallway.

"I doubt it," I lied. It was only a matter of time, really, considering how many infected people we were talking about. If nothing else, they could use brute force to push through. They weren't so good at reasoning, but the brute force part they had down pat. The big thing I didn't want to do was to lead the zombies to the memory care unit of Crofton. That would make getting the supplies in even harder.

Luckily, we got all the way over to the unit without any zombies on our tail. I shifted the boxes over to one arm, knocking with the other. My arms were shaking by this time with all the weight I was holding.

A suspicious voice from inside asked, "Yes?"

I rolled my eyes at Ty, but this time he didn't give me that conspiratorial grin that he usually did. He just looked worried. "It's us," I told the nurse. "Naturally.

Since zombies don't knock."

The woman slowly opened the door and peered out, looking down the long hallway first to ensure that no zombies were shambling toward her. She glanced down at the food that we were holding and her eyes briefly lit up. Then her gaze flickered. "Is this it?"

Ty said, "This is it. This is as much as we could carry and as much as we could get from there."

I was just glad that Ty had been the one to answer. I was getting pretty steamed up by this time with this nurse and I was tired of holding a hundred pounds of food. I raised my foot and kicked the door open wide.

The nurse's mouth was an O of surprise.

Ty and I walked in and set the stuff down right inside the doors. I saw that there were various residents, mostly women, peering from doorways and standing in the hall.

One of them said in a tremulous voice, "Thanks for getting food for us."

I have to admit, this warmed my heart. The nurse had really soured me on the whole getting-food mission and this lady helped remind me that I was actually doing a good deed.

Ty was looking down the hall, trying to see if he could spot his grandmother. The nurse noticed this and said quickly, "What about our medications?"

Her rudeness immediately got under my skin again and my lips tightened to keep from saying what I really thought.

She amended her request, trying to soften it. "As you can see, we're in dire need of help here and you're our only hope."

Well, when she put it that way—

Ty was already heading back to the hall. "Charlie,

let's just get this over with. Then I can catch up with my grandmother after we're done. And find out where Ginny is."

I nodded, but I was thinking everything through. Was this really the best place to offload Ty? The whole place was compromised—the infection was rampant. The food supply was apparently limited to what Ty and I had been able to scavenge and we didn't even know how many residents it was expected to serve. It sounded to me like the better plan was just to find Ty's Nana, convince her to come with us, and leave the facility to find Ty's sister. Then maybe we could find a better location for the three of them to hang out together.

For now, though, I kept my thoughts to myself. The last thing I wanted to do was to complicate the issue. The nurse gave us directions to the infirmary and we set out. This time we left Mojo behind. He wasn't happy about it, but the residents were enchanted with him, so that helped. The infirmary was a different sort of situation, from what we'd seen on the monitor in the office. It looked like there were zombies in the hallway leading up to and past the infirmary. Basically, there was no easy way to get in or get out.

Ty gripped the gun. "Same plan?" he asked in a low voice. "I divert and you grab the medications?"

This plan still gave me heartburn. "I guess. There doesn't seem to be a good way to handle it. But I reserve the right to change the plan in the middle of the mission."

We came up to the spot in the hallway where we needed to make a left turn and head down a different hall. Ty and I kept our backs up against the wall and I carefully peered around the corner.

There was a zombie right there.

I got a split second impression of a disturbing grin from the infected staff member before I barked at Ty to run off and I felt the zombie grab onto me in a surprisingly tight grip and bite down on my forearm as I tried with all my might to push him away.

I heard an alarmed cry from Ty.

"Get out of here!" I yelled to him.

But Ty wasn't listening. As I pulled hard away from the zombie, I heard the gun fire and saw the zombie shoot backward from the impact of the bullet. Finding my chance, I ran back with Ty along the hallway in the direction we'd just come from.

When we got up to the memory care unit, the hall was still deserted. I was panting, as much from the intense feelings coursing through me as from the run. "Hey," I said to Ty between gasps. "Leave me out here. I just wanted to get away from that guy. Now let me stay here. I'm going to turn and I don't want you or your Nana or anybody else around me when I do." The thought that I would start attacking Ty or old folks or anybody at all made me feel physically sick. Or maybe I was feeling physically sick because I was already turning. I wasn't sure.

Ty was already shaking his head and knocking on the door. "Cover that up," he said, motioning to my bloody arm. "We'll get some sheets or towels or something in there to make a tourniquet. But if the nurse sees it, there's no way she'll let you in there."

I said gruffly, this time putting more of an edge in my voice, "Didn't you hear me? Leave me here. You know as well as I do what's going to happen next."

But Ty refused to listen. This was a side to him that I hadn't seen yet. It was a typical bullheaded teen. He knocked at the door again. "Got your meds out here! Open up!"

This wasn't going to go well. For one thing, we didn't have any meds. For another, they were going to find out I'd been attacked by an infected person. The chances of Ty finding out where Ginny was were looking slim. Unless Ty's Nana knew.

The nurse's sour face peered out. "Where is it?"

Ty bulldozed his way through the door, grabbing me by my uninjured arm and pulling me through.

The nurse gaped at me and I noticed too late that the blood was now dripping onto the floor. "You've been bitten!" The expression she turned on Ty was white with fury. "Get him out of here! Immediately!"

"Negative," said Ty coolly. He patted Mojo, who was bounding joyfully around us.

"Where are the medicines?" she hissed.

"In the infirmary. We ran into a problem getting them," I gasped.

"Clearly!" The nurse's eyebrows drew down ferociously. "Since the young man won't see sense, surely you will. For *his* sake," she said, jerking her head in Ty's direction. "Walk out that door."

"You see, I have a plan," said Ty, raising his hand to interrupt her. "Here's my plan." He lifted up the gun and the nurse recoiled. "I'm going to talk to my grandmother. You're going to tell me where Ginny is. I'm going to take Charlie with me and get him bandaged up. If or when Charlie starts turning into one of those *things*, I'll put him out of his misery."

I was filled with relief mingled with gratitude. He had a plan, for sure.

"And no one is going to stop me or tell me that I owe them anything else for that information," said Ty in a measured voice. "Do we understand each other?"

The nurse eyed the weapon and nodded slowly.

"Good," said Ty. "Which room is my grandmother in, since she's not in her regular room?"

The nurse's eyes glinted. "At the end of the hall. Last door on the right."

Ty motioned to me and we walked down the hall. Residents popped back into their rooms as we came toward them. All except the actual memory care residents. The ones that weren't in bed stayed right where they were and stared at us as we hobbled by.

"I'm still not so sure this is a good idea," I mumbled to Ty.

His hand tightened on my arm. "I wasn't leaving you behind. You'd have done the same for me."

He was right, but I still didn't feel good about it. On the way down the hall, Ty stopped by a nurse's station that had a few supplies left. He took a bottle of rubbing alcohol and removed the top. He was looking for cotton balls when I said, "Just pour it right over the top."

Ty winced, but did as instructed. I gritted my teeth at the strong stinging of the alcohol hitting the damaged skin. Then Ty pulled off some gauze and medical tape and quickly helped bandage me up.

"I'm going to stay with you to keep an eye on you," said Ty. We walked briskly to the end of the hall and Ty rapped on the door.

A lady with a sweet smile and somewhat wild hair answered. She beamed at us.

"Nana!" said Ty. He reached for his grandmother and enveloped the small woman with a big hug.

I could see his Nana's face. She gave me a bemused look and I felt that sinking feeling in my stomach that I didn't think had anything to do with the fact that I'd been bitten.

"What a nice boy," she said in a gentle voice,

reaching up a hand to absently rub Ty's hair.

He abruptly leaned back to study his grandmother. "Nana? Are you okay?"

But his grandmother clearly wasn't. She was gazing at Ty with a sort of milky, confused expression. I don't know if she'd been like this for a while and Ty's parents didn't *know*, or if she'd been this way and they just didn't want to tell their kids. Ty was staring at his grandmother in disbelief. Then he gave her a quick hug. "It's okay, Nana. Don't worry."

She gave him a searching look as if trying to place him and seemed worried that she couldn't. Realizing she must be slipping somehow, she asked, "Want to come in for water?"

"No, it's okay." Ty turned to look at me and I could tell he was fighting strong emotion. This had been one of his last hopes—that he could connect with an adult in his family and get some help. To unload some of the burden he was carrying. And now he was put in the position of trying to figure out what to do about his grandmother.

I hesitated. "Ty, I know what you're thinking. But it's bound to be a big risk getting her out of here. She won't grasp the danger and probably won't be able to focus on getting out. She might jeopardize our escape." It was all true. But I knew Ty was loyal. He'd just proved it by insisting I stay with him after I was injured.

I was right. Ty was already shaking his head. "I've got to get Nana out of here. I owe that to her and to my folks." He swallowed hard before continuing. "She's my responsibility. If she and I run into trouble getting out—then just keep going, Charlie."

Then he turned back to his grandmother. "Nana, we need to leave here."

A stubborn expression crossed the old lady's face. "No."

"Nana, it's not safe here. There's not enough food or medicine. You won't get enough care. And there are dangerous—people—here."

"No. I won't leave." There was a determined expression in her eyes.

Ty gently put an arm around his grandmother. "Nana, I love you. I'm going to take care of you and take you to a better place. A safer place."

She pulled away with more strength than I'd thought she had. "I will not leave here. I won't. No."

All Ty's entreaties fell on deaf ears as his grandmother continued shaking her head in response to his every suggestion.

Finally I saw something that approached lucidity—just a glint—in her eyes. She grabbed Ty by his arms and looked up into his face. "I just want it over. I don't want to leave. Don't make me."

Ty gave me a helpless look.

After thinking a moment, I said, "Ty, I don't know. It doesn't seem like a good idea to force her. She's strong still—she can pull back. I don't know how easy it will be to drag or carry her out unwillingly."

He slowly nodded and then gave his grandmother a sad look. "Are you sure, Nana? Really sure?"

But her expression was blank again. Ty pulled her into another embrace before taking a shaky breath. "All right. I won't try to make her leave."

I could tell Ty was right on the brink of losing it. I tried shifting to another topic. I looked around his Nana's makeshift living quarters. Apparently, she'd taken a bag with a bunch of stuff in it from her usual room. There were a couple of photographs and old drawings that I guess Ty and his sister had made years ago. Something else caught my eye.

"Ty," I said, bobbing my head toward a small table. "Doesn't that piece of paper have your name on it?"

Ty swung his head around and stared at the table before striding over to pick it up. "It's Ginny's handwriting!" he said, staring at the looping schoolgirl print.

Ty's grandmother looked worried. "That's very important. Very important."

Ty opened it up and skimmed it. "She says where she's going. And what happened to her and who she's with." He gave me a wide grin—the first one I'd seen in a while and gave his grandmother a tight hug.

Chapter Twenty-Five

Mallory

It wasn't just that Ginny's grandmother didn't recognize Ty's name. Ginny's face was stricken when she realized her grandmother didn't recognize *her*.

I reached out to give her a hug, and then answered for Ginny, "Mrs. Brown, Ty and Ginny here are your grandchildren. We just ran by to check on you and make sure you're okay."

The old lady gave a vague nod. Then she smiled kindly at Ginny. "What a sweet girl. Do you live here, too?"

Ginny looked up at me with tears in her eyes. It was clear to me that Clarice Brown had been slipping into dementia for probably a good while. It also seemed likely that Ginny's parents had decided not to share that information with their children. Maybe they'd kept it secret to keep from upsetting their children. But their approach sure hadn't worked out for the best.

I cleared my throat and said briskly, "Mrs. Brown, now that we've checked in on you, Ginny and I need to go. But what I want to find out is whether you'd like to come with us or not."

Ginny gave my hand a grateful squeeze. I wasn't sure that Clarice Brown would want to leave, but I wanted to at least give her the option. Plus, I wasn't sure how well she could fend for herself here, or who might be available to take care of her.

Ginny's grandmother nodded thoughtfully as if she were carefully considering the choice. Then she said, "I want to stay."

"Are you sure, Nana? You can come with us. We're going to try to find Ty." Ginny seemed to have trouble saying Ty's name. I knew her hopes were high that he'd be here at Crofton.

Her grandmother turned that blank, confused look on Ginny at the mention of Ty. She mumbled, "I want to stay."

Right then there was a tap at the door and we turned to see a thin nurse standing there. Her lips were pressed together in disapproval and her face was lined with stress. "It's you," she said brusquely. "I guess you made your way in."

This was the woman who'd opened the gate for us then. I looked at her coolly.

The nurse glanced at Mrs. Brown. "We need to move you now," she said. "Really, we should have moved you weeks ago, but we were trying to give your family time to help you."

Clarice Brown gazed uncomprehendingly at her.

I said, "Where are you moving Mrs. Brown? Surely business isn't carrying on as usual right now."

The nurse pursed her lips again. "It certainly isn't. But I want to make it easier on myself since I'm really the only staff left. I'm moving all the remaining residents to the memory care unit. It's secured and can be locked from the inside as well as the outside." She studied Mrs. Brown. "And, of course, Mrs. Brown should have been placed in the unit weeks ago."

Ginny frowned. "So she won't be in her room? Won't that be confusing for her?"

"She's already confused," snapped the nurse.

I'd had just about enough from this woman but I was trying to keep from flying off the handle since I felt that was the last thing Ginny needed right now. "I'll put some things together and carry them over to the memory unit. It might help her get more adjusted there."

"And you are?" the nurse tried to look down her nose at me, but since she was shorter than I was, it didn't work well.

"I'm a friend of Ginny's. And Ginny is Clarice Brown's granddaughter. Mrs. Brown has decided to stay put and not travel with us," I said.

Ginny's voice was amazingly steady when she spoke to the nurse. "If my brother Ty comes looking for me, can you tell him that I'm safe? And that I have a new friend, Mallory, who is looking after me?"

The nurse gazed noncommittally at her. "I'll see what I can do."

"And that we're going to the Virginia border to a safe house? Crepe Myrtle Lane." Ginny's whole body was tense from her urgency.

The nurse nodded. Then she glanced over at me. "Whatever you need to get out of here, do it fast. I'm bolting those doors at the memory care unit and then I'm not opening them again. Not for anybody."

She left as swiftly as she'd arrived. Ginny's eyes were troubled. I pulled the comforter off the bed and started loading some of Mrs. Brown's things in it to lug it away. To Ginny I said, "You know, I trust that nurse about as far as I can throw her. Why don't you leave a note for Ty? Tell him what's going on. Leave it with your Nana's things. If he comes to Crofton, he'll be looking for your grandmother and will be sure to see the note."

"Do you think so?" Ginny looked hopeful. It was the first time in a while that she'd looked that way.

I smiled at her. "I know so."

While Ginny quickly wrote out a note, I grabbed photos, kids' drawings, and other mementos that might help Mrs. Brown settle in better. When I finished, Ginny was also done. I lightly touched Mrs. Brown's sleeve. "Why don't you follow us?"

"I don't want to leave," the old lady repeated. But she looked bereft as if she knew things were changing and couldn't figure out why.

"I know you don't. But you won't be going far. Just down the hall. I'll set everything up for you," I said softly.

Mrs. Brown put out an arthritic hand and touched my cheek. "Thank you."

As we got Ginny's grandmother moved into the memory care unit, I couldn't help but guiltily realize my relief at keeping Ginny with me. The little girl now almost felt like a daughter to me. At this point, I couldn't even imagine facing the uncertain journey ahead of me without her.

After leaving Crofton (watching our backs the whole time since the contagion seemed to be getting worse by the minute), I drove straight up to the North Carolina/Virginia border. No stopping. We got there in the late afternoon and I felt a huge feeling of relief as I saw the house. It was there and it hadn't changed.

It was a log cabin with solar panels on the roof, an extensive garden at the side of the house, and rain barrels for water collection. I hadn't remembered how the house was positioned and if it was easily defensible or not. And it was really weird to even be thinking about houses in those terms, anyway.

Ginny, drowsy next to me in the front seat, perked up when I slowed the car down. "Are we here?" She sat up straight in her seat and looked out the window. "I love it!"

It looked ... safe. Despite its compactness and the fact that it was a small three bedroom cabin, it had a sturdiness and a no-nonsense look about it that made you feel like you were going to be okay.

"It has a garden on the side of the house and probably still has power, since it's got solar panels. It even has a generator that we can run. My friends really put a lot of time planning it," I said.

Ginny was still looking excitedly out at the house and so she didn't catch my swift change of expression. I'd caught some movement out of the corner of my eye, near the woods. Ginny had been through plenty today and I had, too. I didn't feel much like going on high alert right now. And, luckily, when I scanned the woods, I didn't see anything. Maybe my imagination was starting to run away with me. Or exhaustion.

"Are your friends there, do you think?" asked Ginny. "Annie and Jim?"

It was a good question. I didn't see either car right now. I said, "I'm not sure. Let's go ahead and bring some of our things in and we'll find out. You'll like them ... they're terrific people. Annie makes this amazing zucchini pasta." Ginny wrinkled her nose and I laughed. "You'll love it, I promise."

Ginny opened the door and pulled out some bags from the backseat. "Can we get in if they're not here? Do you have a key?"

"I've got a code for the lock box on the front door." In a moment of panic, I searched the back of my hand where I'd written it just days ago. It felt like months had gone by. I gave a relieved sigh when I spotted the faint 4474 on my skin.

I unlocked the front door and Ginny and I walked in.

"Whoa! This is so cute!" said Ginny.

I smiled at her enthusiasm, but was still thinking about what I had or hadn't seen in the woods. "Isn't it great? I've only been here a couple of times, but I loved it. Annie and Jim live in DC and they think of this place as their getaway." Annie, despite being a corporate attorney, was an earth mama at heart. The cabin was decorated with blankets, place mats, chair cushions, and potholders that she'd stitched by hand over the years, all in a cheerful checkered pattern.

But where *were* Annie and Jim? It had been Annie's plan to come here, and she'd sounded like she was either on her way out or close to it. I felt an uneasiness in the pit of my stomach which I disguised in light conversation with Ginny as we got everything out of the car and brought it in. I kept watching the woods, but didn't see anything.

After we'd unpacked, Ginny said, "Is it okay with you if I go take a long bath? I just kept thinking that would be the best thing in the world when I was out in the woods—if I could just have a nice, hot bath."

I smiled at her and nodded. "Of course you can. We're celebrating getting here, aren't we? While you're in there, I'll think about what we can eat."

But the first thing I did when Ginny disappeared happily into the bathroom was to peer into the garage. And I saw Annie's Volkswagen Bug in there. I stared at it for a few moments, trying to digest what this meant.

I knew that Annie didn't leave a car down here while she was in D.C. So it must mean that she was here somewhere. But she wasn't in the house. I shivered, thinking about the movement I'd thought I'd spotted in the woods.

I firmly locked the doors. Then, just to make sure, I pushed chairs in front of the doors. I closed the curtains. Then I did poke around in the kitchen to see what I could make for a quick dinner. I found unopened boxes of cereal and unopened fully cooked bacon strips. Breakfast for supper? Why not? That was always a comfort food for me and right now I needed some comfort.

Ginny came back out, squeaky clean, and smiling. "I smell bacon!"

We did indeed have power—I wasn't sure if it came from a power plant or from the solar panels on the roof. For the next hour, though, I put all my worries about Annie and everything else out of my mind and focused on having a fun evening with Ginny. Finally, she gave a huge yawn and said, "I'm going to enjoy a real bed now. Goodnight."

"Goodnight," I said to her with a lightness that I didn't really feel as the light grew dimmer outside.

It was a couple of hours before I fell into a fitful sleep. In my dream, I was buried underground and scratching frantically with my fingernails to try and dig my way back out. I woke up gasping. Then I realized that I still heard a scratching sound.

My heart pounded as I followed the noise to the back of the house. Moving slowly, I listened for the scratching sound until I ended up at the back door. Catching my breath, I spotted a dark form scratching at the wood and glass of the door.

It was Annie. Or, it used to be Annie. Her usually clever, laughing eyes were hollow orbs and her mouth hung slackly. When she saw me, she moaned and her empty eyes grew larger and she pounded her hands on the door.

I jerked away and ran to pull a sofa in front of the door. I covered up the window portion of the door by duct taping a blanket over it. I was perspiring like crazy at this point, shaking with revulsion and sadness and fear.

I headed for the front of the house again, figuring if I left that the creature that had been Annie would leave, too. But I knew one thing. I wanted to arm myself. It hadn't seemed that important at the start of this whole thing, but now I had Ginny with me. I wanted to keep Ginny safe. And Annie, in her normal state, would want the same thing.

Jim had been too much of an animal lover to be a hunter, but I remembered him saying that he did keep a gun here as a "just in case." Mostly because the area was so remote that he felt he needed something for protection since it would take the sheriff an hour or more to get out here. And now, of course, who even knew if the sheriff would, or even *could*, come at all.

I gave up on sleeping for the time being and went right to the master bedroom. I searched the bedside tables and under the bed and finally the neatly organized closet. That's where I found the gun safe. Typical Jim—he'd carefully locked it up. But where was the key?

After some more searching, I located the key in a pair of shoes at the top of the closet. I opened the gun safe and found a loaded .22.

It had been a while since I'd been shooting. I'd been raised by my father—my mother had died in a car accident before I could really even form memories of her. But my father, now dead himself from cancer, made sure that I would have the ability to defend myself if I needed to. I was the only twelve year old girl at the shooting range. He taught me gun safety and the preciousness of human life and the responsibility of gun ownership.

Now I stared at the gun and tried to remember everything he'd taught me. One thing I knew—when it came right down to it—I wouldn't hesitate to shoot if I was defending Ginny.

I was awake the rest of the night. How could I sleep? Once the sun started coming up, I pulled the curtain back on a front window just enough to be able to look out. For hours, I saw nothing but birds and squirrels and even an occasional deer. They went about their normal activities as if there was nothing to worry about, nothing different about their world.

And then I heard the sound of motors and I tensed again. Someone was on their way into the driveway.

Chapter Twenty-Six

Ty

I felt better about life for the first time in days. After we left Crofton, even though I hated leaving Nana behind, I knew where we were heading. I knew Ginny was, most likely all right. And I felt good about where we were traveling. Ginny was usually a good judge of character, and she liked this Mallory lady. For the first time in a while, I felt pretty optimistic.

We drove overnight, although we did have to stop for gas. Then we stopped again at another small town that looked deserted, but had a local grocery store. The ground was flat and there weren't many buildings, so we felt safe going in and getting more supplies. At this point, we had so much stuff in the truck that we even put some things in the front seat next to Mojo.

Charlie motioned to me that he wanted to pull over. It was dawn by this point. When I pulled over, I saw he was tinkering with his phone. I rolled my window down. "Do we still have a connection?" I asked.

He shrugged, looking down at the device. "It comes and goes. I'm just trying to get GPS to come up for long enough to get a lock on my location and that address your sister gave you. Just so I can jot it down real quick."

We waited another couple of minutes while

Charlie fussed at the phone and gave long sighs. Then he lit up. "Finally!" He swiped at his phone a few times to get the turn by turn instructions while writing them down. "Okay, it doesn't look far. And there aren't enough roads for us to really get lost."

I gave him a thumbs-up and he grinned at me and started the bike back up. Mojo, who always got restless when we were stopped, relaxed again and even took a nap on the last part of our trip.

It was daytime by the time Charlie pointed down a driveway, letting me know we'd gotten to Crepe Myrtle Lane. But I was so pumped that I wasn't even tired. The gravel driveway curved through the woods and up to a log cabin with solar panels on the roof, and a full garden. I started to smile. Plus, the thought of actually being back in a bed again sounded pretty good.

Charlie was already off his bike and I was opening the car door when the sound of a gun going off made us jump. Charlie muttered, "What's going on? I know I put the right address in."

"Maybe the lady taking care of Ginny doesn't recognize you and she's worried. Maybe it was just a warning shot," I said, although my heart sank. We'd come too far to run into trouble now. Now we weren't expecting it and that made it tougher.

Instead of sitting back down in the truck, I stepped away from it with my hands high.

"Are you crazy?" asked Charlie. "I'm thinking we need to get out of here, pronto."

I called out, being careful to be loud enough to be heard, but not loud enough to draw attention from any zombies that might be in the area. "Is Mallory here? It's Ty. Ginny's brother. I'm with a friend of mine."

The front door burst open and Ginny sped toward me, tears running down her cheeks.

We didn't say anything, couldn't really say anything. We just held each other in a tight, tight hug.

Charlie reached out a hand to Ginny when we'd finally stopped hugging. "Ginny, I presume?" he asked with a grin, giving a low bow that made her giggle. "I'm Charlie."

"Nice to meet you. And that's Mallory, up there," said Ginny, motioning to the house.

Mallory was standing stiffly on the porch, still holding a .22 that was very similar to Charlie's. She said in a gruff voice, "Maybe we should make our introductions and have our reunions inside." She quickly walked in, seeming uncomfortable with the scene.

Charlie murmured, "Whatever you say, as long as you're not shooting at me." He ambled toward the house, giving a short whistle to Mojo, who jumped out the passenger window to follow him. "Hey, I'm bringing a German shepherd in. Is that okay?" he called.

Ginny was already reaching out for Mojo, burying her face in his fur.

"I see he's already made a friend," said Charlie.

Mojo bounded beside Ginny up to the cabin. I saw that Mallory was looking watchfully out the door, but not at us—at the woods. I shivered a little and glanced behind me. I didn't see anything. I don't think Mallory did either, but she was still scanning. That made me wonder.

Charlie didn't seem to notice that Mallory looked worried. That's because he was stealing these sort of sideways glances at her. But he probably could have just outright stared at her because she wasn't paying him the slightest bit of attention.

Still, as soon as I came into the cabin, she gave

me a smile that made her eyes crinkle. "Ty, I've heard a lot about you. You don't know how *happy* we are to see you."

I did, though. Ginny was doing a happy dance inside the cabin, not able to really settle down. And I could tell that Mallory was glad too, even though she was tense. Too tense to really register Charlie. Charlie probably wasn't too used to that. He wasn't like a movie star or a male model or anything, but he was a real guy and a good looking one with his tan and his dark hair. Tall, dark, and handsome, wasn't that what they said? He was all of those things.

Mallory was definitely distracted. And there had been that thing with the gun, too. Something had made her nervous and wary.

She seemed to suddenly remember that she hadn't really given us a warm welcome when we'd arrived. "Ah, sorry about the gun thing." She watched as Ginny chased after Mojo into the back of the cabin. Mallory added in a low, quick voice, "Ginny had had a run-in with some guys that had hijacked Ty's van and thought about kidnapping her, too. So I guess I'm just jumpy."

My eyes opened wide. I wasn't sure what I *thought* might have happened to Ginny, but getting the van stolen from her and being threatened wasn't something that I'd considered. "Was she—was she okay when you found her?"

Mallory nodded quickly and gave me a reassuring smile. "You've got a tough sister, Ty. She was shaken up, but she was fine. And we hit it off really well."

I nodded. "It looks like it. Did you—well—was she okay when she saw our grandmother?"

"It was tough for her. She obviously didn't know that your grandmother was experiencing any memory loss." Mallory paused. "Did you know?"

I shook my head. "I guess Mom and Dad didn't have a chance to tell us. Or maybe they didn't want us to worry. Plus, sometimes they weren't really good at keeping us in the loop. I felt bad about leaving her there."

Mallory said, "Don't. Because if your grandmother was anything like she was when Ginny and I were there, she wasn't going anywhere, anyway."

Charlie had been spending time looking around the cabin a little bit and now joined us again as Ginny and Mojo were playing with a tennis ball Charlie had found in one of the bedrooms.

Charlie said, "So, is this your country retreat, Mallory?" He tilted his head to the side questioningly.

Mallory's defenses seemed like they were back up. "No. No, actually, it belongs to my friends. Annie and Jim are friends of mine from way back. They live in D.C. and then came out here on weekends and for vacations. I think they had a guy who was sort of a caretaker who came out some and took care of things around here while they were gone."

Charlie nodded. "That makes sense. I saw some pictures around the cabin and I didn't see any of you. Have you been in touch with Annie and Jim?"

Mallory got a little prickly. "They know I'm here, if that's what you mean."

Charlie raised his eyebrows but made his tone softer. "I wasn't worried about that. Heck, I've taken to looting stores. It's a whole new world. I was just trying to get a handle on where your friends might be and if they would be cool with a few extra guests, that's all."

I thought this might make Mallory relax a little, but instead she seemed even more tense. "They're not the kinds to worry about extra guests. They wouldn't even think of you as guests at all—they'd make you feel like you were family. The only problem is, I don't know where they are."

She cast a look behind her to make sure Ginny wasn't coming in and then she said, "I was trying not to tell Ginny, because she was so glad about being in a safer place. It's true that I don't know what happened to Jim. I have the feeling he must not have been able to make it out of D.C. But I think Annie made it all the way here. And was attacked." Mallory took a deep breath.

Charlie sat abruptly down on the arm of the checkered sofa. "You've seen her, you mean? You're sure it was her?"

Mallory swallowed. "Positive. And her car is in the garage. But this place is so remote. We've been thinking of it as a safe place. I can't think who would have attacked her here."

"Maybe the caretaker," I said. I understood why Mallory wouldn't want to tell Ginny. For me, though, I'd never built this cabin up as a "safe place." I was believing there were no "safe places" anymore.

Charlie obviously believed the same thing. "We need to be alert. But we can't spend every day barricaded in the house." He glanced around at the drawn curtains and blocked doors.

Mallory looked away. "I know that. I think it was mainly for my benefit. I couldn't handle seeing my best friend like that."

Charlie's face softened and it looked like he was about to reach out for Mallory to give her comfort. But she quickly glanced up, frowning, and his hand dropped again. For some reason, these two didn't seem to be hitting it off. Which was a pain, because I liked both of them and didn't want there to be a bunch of tension in the house. I had gotten enough of that at home with my parents.

The rest of the day, we settled in. Charlie and I moved all of our stuff out of the truck and into the cabin. We did keep one eye on the woods, but didn't see anything. Luckily, the cabin had plenty of storage space in the closets, the attic, and pantry. We settled in, putting some of our stuff away. It was a three-bedroom house and, since Mallory didn't think her friends were probably going to be back, Ginny and I took the room with the bunk beds, Mallory took one bedroom, and Charlie took the other.

That afternoon, Mallory loosened up a little bit. But whenever Charlie would say something to her, she'd always get that tenseness in her shoulders again. I didn't really get it, since Charlie was being nice and she didn't even know him. But it made me wonder if she'd had a bad experience with a guy recently and was still trying to recover from that. Plus, of course, her whole life had been turned upside down in the last few days, just like everybody else's.

After we'd eaten some canned vegetables for supper, Charlie rolled his sleeves up to wash the dishes. And that's when Mallory *really* got tense.

"What's that?" she asked, staring at his arm. Then her eyes narrowed. "You've been bitten." She looked like she wanted to grab Ginny and lock them both up in the back of the house.

Charlie sighed. "I should have said something. We were just so focused on getting here and then getting settled in. Yes, I was bitten when we were at the retirement home yesterday. But I haven't had any kind of issue although the bite hurt like crazy."

Ginny's eyes were huge. "Are you okay?"

Mallory said harshly, "I can't believe you'd put us

all at risk like that."

"I'd *never* put anyone at risk. That's totally against my nature," said Charlie.

"But you stayed with Ty after you were infected," said Mallory.

Now Charlie was starting to look irritated. "I wasn't infected. I was just bitten."

"You couldn't have known that you weren't going to be infected, though. You *should* have been infected. Everyone else was," said Mallory.

"He tried to stay behind," I said firmly. "He told me to leave him there, outside the safe area of Crofton. But I wouldn't do it because he wouldn't have done it if it had been me. Besides, everyone else got infected immediately after being scratched or bitten. Charlie was fine. And he'd given me a gun, just in case he wasn't fine later."

"Did you know how to shoot it, though?" pressed Mallory.

"I did and do," I said.

She thought about this for a minute. About what I'd said about Charlie. Every once in a while she'd glance up at him as if trying to size him up. Charlie started soaping up dishes, rinsing them off, and putting them in the drainer.

"It doesn't make sense, though," she finally muttered. "Why wouldn't you get infected like everyone else? What's different about you?"

If it had just been Charlie and me together, he'd probably have made some kind of joke about all the ways he was different. But he took the question seriously as he was finishing up with washing a glass.

"I wonder if it had something to do with my vaccinations," he said slowly.

"Vaccinations?" asked Mallory.

"Yeah. I'd just changed jobs. I was tired of being a salesman. Always on, you know. Always Mr. Personality."

I saw Mallory nod a little, as if she could understand that.

"I wanted to have a job where I really felt like I could help people and make a difference. I know that sounds cheesy," he said with a little laugh. "But after selling a software product for years to corporations that probably didn't even need it, I needed a real change. So I decided to become a paramedic. Huge career change."

Mallory raised her eyebrows in agreement.

"Anyway, I ended up having to get tons of immunizations. Some of them were boosters, some were totally new and different from the shots I'd gotten as a kid."

"And you think that one of those vaccinations might have given you some kind of immunity," she murmured.

"Maybe," said Charlie with a shrug as he leaned back against the sink. "The tetanus maybe? Who knows? But it's the only thing that makes a little bit of sense."

"There are tons of people who have updated tetanus shots, though. Like me," said Mallory slowly.

"Right. But I *just had* mine. Maybe it has something to do with the amount of time the vaccination is in the bloodstream. I'm not a scientist or a doctor, so I'm just throwing out guesses. For now, though, I'm going to be a party pooper and hit the sack," said Charlie. "The last couple of days have worn me out." He hesitated. "I'm not anticipating any problems, but if anything happens tonight or if anybody needs me at all, just come wake me up. I might sleep pretty hard since I'm so exhausted."

Mallory considered him thoughtfully. I thought I saw a little bit of the ice thawing. She nodded.

Chapter Twenty-Seven

Charlie

I couldn't remember where I was when I was waking up the next morning so I had that kind of startled, confused, alarmed feeling that made me sit straight up in bed.

Once I realized I was in the cabin, I relaxed a little. It did feel like a safe place. Safer even than that house in the woods I'd gone to earlier. I knew Mallory was still worried that her friend was lurking around, waiting to attack., but I knew one thing: I felt pretty good about fighting off one zombie. It was the city of zombies or the retirement home full of zombies that I didn't feel so confident about.

Mallory was something else I didn't feel so confident about. I'd felt an immediate pull toward her when I'd first seen her. She was strong, smart, and beautiful. And probably a good twelve years younger than I was. She was way out of my league—in a normal world. But this was the zombie apocalypse, where there were different possibilities. That was, as a matter of fact, the *only* good thing about the zombie apocalypse—that we could experience a totally different reality.

It was obvious, though, that Mallory had put major barriers up. She was uncomfortable around me. She tensed up when I entered the room. As somebody who's gone through divorce and experienced how bad a relationship can get, I saw some of the same characteristics in Mallory. She acted like someone who'd been hurt. Like somebody reluctant to trust again. I could get that. And there was one thing I knew I had in my favor—time. As long as Annie the Zombie didn't get me, that was. Although, considering I'd already survived one attack, I was feeling a bit more optimistic about my chances.

I decided that actions spoke louder than words. If I wanted Mallory to trust me, I should behave in a trustworthy, adult manner. I decided to scrounge up breakfast from the hodgepodge of stuff we had accumulated here.

After a quick perusal of the food, I decided to treat us with some of the breakfast MREs. They were actually tasty, unlike some of the other MREs. And, since they took no time to prepare, I had breakfast ready in minutes.

Ginny was the first one up. "Can I feed Mojo?" she asked shyly.

I really liked Ginny. She seemed like an awesome kid. A lot of middle school kids had issues, but I saw no sign of any in Ginny, which was pretty amazing, considering everything she'd gone through. And I'd kind of gotten the impression from Ty that the kids' home life hadn't been exactly easy, either. "Sure thing! He'll be your friend for life. As a matter of fact, I think he's your friend for life anyway."

"What should I give him? Is there any dog food?"

"That's sort of an unfortunate thing. There isn't any dog food in there. But we've got some canned soup in there. I bet he'll eat a meaty soup. Then, later on, I'll figure something out for Mojo. Maybe he can eat squirrel or possum or something."

Ginny wrinkled her nose at the thought of squirrel and possum.

The dog had clearly fallen for Ginny. His amber eyes were full of love as she found a large can of soup and poured it in a bowl she found in a cabinet.

I knew I shouldn't quiz Ginny on Mallory, but I couldn't seem to help myself. I glanced to the back to make sure Mallory wouldn't pop up and hear me pumping Ginny for information. I handed a plate of food to her and then asked in a low voice, "So you and Mallory have gotten to be good friends, right?"

Ginny nodded, smiling at Mojo as he decimated the bowl of soup. "Right."

"What do you think of her? I mean, did she talk about herself at all or her background?"

Ginny considered this for a minute. "I really like her. She's almost like a much-older sister or a cool aunt or something. But she didn't talk about herself much. I think she worked in government, but I don't know anything else. I just know that she saved my life. She stopped her car when she didn't have to and let me ride with her. There's no way I'd have made it without her."

Ginny was starting to get that haunted look, which made me realize that she didn't need to revisit the moment when she and Ty got separated.

I quickly changed the subject. "She sure does seem really great. Hey, do you know how to play cards?"

She laughed at the swift subject change. "Only Old Maid. And Crazy Eights. Maybe Go Fish."

"No, no, no," I said in mock horror. "I meant *real* card games. Like poker."

"Nope. No poker. Ty knows how to play, though. Sometimes he plays with his high school friends."

"Well, when I was in the back bedroom, I found a couple of decks of cards. What do you think about learning how to play well enough so you can beat your brother?"

Her eyes lit up. "Show me."

So for the next hour or so, I showed her how to play the game. Ginny and I joked around a lot during the process. It was fun and I hadn't had real fun in a long while.

I looked up at one point and saw that Mallory was in the doorway, watching us with an expression I really couldn't read. I wondered how long she'd been studying us.

Ginny saw the direction of my gaze and said, "Hi Mallory! Charlie is showing me how to win at poker."

"It's a survival skill in the new world," I said with a smile.

I saw just a hint of a smile from Mallory at me before she gave Ginny a full grin. "Sounds like you'll be beating me, then. I haven't played since college."

I quickly stood up and handed Mallory a plate of food. "Breakfast for you, madam," I said with a mock bow.

She gave me a slightly reproving look, although I could tell she was starting to melt a little. Unless it was just wishful thinking on my part.

"Thanks," she said, quickly looking away. "Ginny, catch me up to speed on poker so I won't lose too badly."

"Don't you do it, Ginny!" I said. "Make her learn by losing."

It was good to have that sort of banter happening. It helped make the horror of the last week get pushed into the background a little.

A few minutes later, Ty was up. "Could you guys

be any louder?" he asked sleepily, looking and sounding like a normal teenage boy for the first time since I met him. I was glad to see the teen side—he'd been way too mature for his age and had too much responsibility. Life and death responsibility.

"Want some breakfast?" Mallory asked. "Charlie made it for us."

To my surprise, Ty shook his head. "No appetite this morning, sorry. Maybe later on."

I said, "You *are* a teenage boy, right?"

He smiled at me. "Yeah, but I can't eat when I first wake up. Need to move around some first."

Ginny said, "Ty, want to throw the ball outside for Mojo with me?"

Mallory froze. I could tell she cared a lot for Ginny and didn't want her even thinking about being outside. If she had her way, Ginny would probably stay inside the barricaded house—safe and secure—for years.

The thing was, though, that since she had decided not to share her concerns with Ginny, Ginny saw no reason *not* to go outside. Because this house had been billed as a safe house by Mallory herself.

Ginny frowned, uncertain why no one was answering and why everyone had gotten tense all of a sudden. "Is something wrong?"

"Nothing's wrong," I said lightly, "except for your brother's odd disinterest in food, that is. Go on outside. Mojo will love it."

Ty glanced back and forth between Mallory and me, trying to get a feel for what he should do. When Ginny had gone into the back of the house to get the ball, I mimed a gun, indicating that he should take it with him. "And be sure to keep an eye out," I added in a low voice.

Ty gave a quick nod and a couple of minutes later

he and his sister and an excited Mojo ran outside.

Mallory was strained and silent again and I hated that it seemed like we'd lost any of the ground we'd made that morning. I cleared my throat. "Mojo is real good about pinpointing zombie activity. He can smell them from a huge distance away. And you can't miss it when he does because he starts growling and his fur stands up on his back."

Mallory sighed. "I just don't want them out there. Not considering what I saw."

"I know it's got to be tough on you, Mallory. It's been a really rough week," I said in my most understanding voice. Although I didn't actually completely understand—I just *wanted* to.

"You think you understand, but you don't," she said almost absently as she stared out the window at the kids playing.

"You're right. Then tell me what's wrong," I urged.

She gave a harsh laugh. "What's *wrong*? What *isn't* wrong? I see a new friend of mine get attacked by zombies as he tries rescuing me. I see a girl who was almost kidnapped and taken away by a gang. I experience a retirement home overrun with zombies. And my best friend in the world is hanging around me in the hopes of attacking me."

I was quiet for a few moments and then said, "If it helps at all, remember that these infected people *aren't* thinking at all. They're just reacting. It's not like Annie wishes you harm in any way. And I know you've gone through a nightmare. We've *all* gone through a nightmare. But it seems to me like there's something more. Maybe something that happened before the infection started."

Mallory still stared through the window, this time looking blankly out it and not really seeming to see the kids.

I said, "I went through a divorce pretty recently. I know what it's like to get hurt in a relationship."

She gave that hard laugh again. "Not like this."

"I'm sure that's true. But all I want is to be friends," I lied. "I want to have a stress-free environment for us all to relax in. Because it sure as heck ain't stress-free out there," I said, motioning out the window. "Can we have a truce?"

Mallory hesitated and looked at the hand I had outstretched for her to shake. Slowly, she reached out to shake it. "It wasn't about you," she said softly.

"I know that," I said with a smile. "Because you don't even know me."

It got a little easier from that point. We had a good working relationship for the next couple of weeks. But it wasn't exactly what I wanted from Mallory. I wanted more.

Chapter Twenty-Eight

Mallory

Like anything new, it took a few weeks for me to feel like I'd really settled in at Crepe Myrtle Lane. For one thing, Annie's appearance had totally unnerved me and the fact that I hadn't seen her since didn't exactly make me relieved. It only meant that she was still out there somewhere.

I saw exactly why Ginny was such a fan of her brother. Ty was a great kid and completely changed my opinion of teens. He was mature and capable and a hard worker.

And Charlie seemed warm and funny and smart. The only problem was me. I had this huge emotional and mental barrier I had to somehow get past. My relationship with Brendan had been damaging in many ways and one of those ways was the fact it eroded my ability to trust. I was working to get over it, but it was tough.

One day, a few weeks after we'd moved in, Ty went out for his shift of weed pulling and crop watering and Ginny was tossing the ball to a joyful Mojo. It was a hot summer day and I was trying to clean our dirty laundry by hand so that I could hang it outside and dry it. Charlie was in the front yard, building more shelves so we could better organize food and other supplies.

My blood ran cold when I heard it. A sharp,

alarmed, throaty warning bark from Mojo and a piercing scream from Ginny. Everyone was outside, so with shaking hands I found the gun that I hadn't shot since the day Ty and Charlie joined us.

I yanked open the door and saw Mojo lunging back and forth between Ginny and the back of a disfigured, gaunt form dressed in an outfit that I recognized. Annie. And Annie, or what had been Annie, was standing between Ginny and the safety of the house.

Charlie ran around the side of the house and stopped at the sight. Ty quickly joined him. "Ginny! Run into the woods!"

But like a bad nightmare, Ginny seemed immobile, eyes fixed in horror at the creature that had been my friend. I remembered she'd done much the same when we'd seen the zombie woman at the shack in the woods.

Charlie said, "Mallory, unlock the front door and I'll come in and grab the gun."

"There's no time," I said, suddenly feeling a calmness and a certainty that I hadn't felt in a long while. This was something I needed to do. And Annie wouldn't have had it any other way.

"Ginny, you don't have to try to run," I said in a measured tone. "I know you're shaking and scared. Just move to your right."

Ginny, white-faced, stumbled off to the right with Mojo backing up to protectively hover in front of her, showing his teeth.

With a strength, resolve, and ability that seemed to come from nowhere, I jogged up closer to Annie so there would be no misses and no accidental friendly fire toward anyone else, and pointing the gun at her head, put her down.

Then I was the one shaking. Hard. Silent tears ran down my face. But when Charlie folded me into his embrace, I finally felt myself really relax and release all of the fear, mistrust, and hurt into his capable hands. The past was in the past.

Ginny and Ty both joined in our embrace and from that point on, we were a family.

Epilogue

Mallory

In some ways, I'd never felt safer in my life. I had a real family for the first time. People who actually cared for each other and worked for a real purpose— sustainability. There were some days, it's true, that I didn't *want* to feel like a pioneer family and grow crops, weed, and can and chop wood for fuel. But I got something out of it that I didn't get when I was working in government: a feeling of purpose. And I think Charlie felt the same way. It's why he quit sales in the first place.

Ty had become a good hunter and I soon started feeling more relaxed about him and Charlie heading off into the woods to hunt. I even showed them what Joshua had taught me about snare hunting. Every once in a while there would be a lone infected soul that would wander into our patch and they'd be quickly taken out. We all agreed that was the best way to handle infected people: it was the most humane approach for them and for us. Although I wonder if I ever really got over poor Annie.

The seeds that Ty took from the country store ended up coming in particularly handy and we all learned a lot about gardening.

There was, in some ways, a sameness to the days, although I did track them on a homemade calendar since old habits die hard. It was for this reason that I knew it had been several months after our arrival at the house when we got an unexpected, *live,* visitor.

It was a late spring evening when there was a knock at our door right after we'd finished supper. We froze, even though we knew zombies didn't knock. They might scratch sometimes, but they never rapped on a door with such authority. Just to be on the safe side, Ty had a hand on his gun as Charlie and I answered the door.

There was a very nonthreatening-looking man wearing a short-sleeved button-down shirt with a couple of pens in the pocket. He had heavy glasses and sturdy walking shoes and carried a briefcase. He looked every bit the role of a mild-mannered accountant of some kind.

"Good evening," he said briskly, reaching in his briefcase and pulling out a legal pad and removing a pen out of his pocket. He glanced behind him. "Are your woods safe or should I come inside?"

"And you are—?" asked Charlie in a friendly but still wary voice. You just never knew these days. As innocuous as this guy appeared, you really just never knew.

"Sorry," he said, pulling out a business card and presenting it to us. "I'm Arthur Wilson, a census taker for the United States Government. I'm taking a special census to determine surviving pockets of uninfected people and where they're centered. Additionally, I'm also supplying information to these possibly isolated pockets."

I felt Ginny's hand on mine and I gave it a little squeeze to let her know everything was okay.

"In that case," I said, "Please come inside. It's

safe out there, yes, but you're probably ready for a break from the road."

The man bobbed his head in thanks and trotted in, settling himself at a desk in the front room. "So there are four of you here? Are you an intact family or a created family?"

As we answered all his census questions, the questions and our answers reminded me once again how much things had changed in this new world. The new normal was radically different from the old one.

When Arthur had finished with his questions, he carefully closed his legal pad and put his pen back into his pocket. He was starting to stand when Charlie raised his hand. "Whoa, whoa, whoa," he said in that friendly but still authoritative voice. "Now we need some information in return."

"Of course," said the little man, quickly. He sat back down, folded his hands in his lap, and prepared to deliver a speech he'd apparently given quite a few times before. Clearing his throat, he opened his mouth and then rapidly closed it again, staring at Charlie. "Excuse me, but are those scars from a bite?"

"More than one bite, I'd say," answered Charlie coolly.

"From an Infected," continued Arthur, raptly staring at the scars.

"That's right. If that's what you call them," said Charlie.

"With absolutely no repercussions. That is, you were not harmed."

"Well, I wouldn't say *absolutely no* repercussions, because it hurt like heck and I had to put all kinds of ointments and bandages on it. But if you mean repercussions like, did I start going around savagely attacking people, then no," said Charlie a bit impatiently now.

"Very interesting," breathed the census taker. "I've actually come across only a couple of you in my travels, although there are rumors among the census takers that there are quite a few more. We're to ask a separate list of questions whenever we come across such a specimen."

He carefully flipped to the correct page of his notebook for these questions while Charlie rolled his eyes at us. I hid a smile, but Ty and Ginny couldn't resist grinning.

Arthur's questions all related to Charlie's vaccinations and when he'd received them. Charlie waggled his eyebrows at me. He'd been right. There appeared to be a connection.

"Very interesting," repeated the census taker at the completion of the questions. "Very interesting indeed."

"So does this mean that the US Government is working on a vaccine program to help prevent infection from spreading?" I asked.

Arthur pursed his lips. "I don't like to speculate on the workings of the US Government. It's working at quite a reduced capacity, as you can imagine. It's taking a while to gather information, too, obviously. Once they are able to secure and operate the power grid on at least a reduced basis, perhaps everyone will be able to log in to this census and make things go a bit faster. But yes, my understanding is that they're planning to launch a vaccine program—but they want to make sure they understand where all the pockets of people are who would require such immunizations."

Charlie said, "And the other information you've got for us?"

Arthur sat up a bit straighter in his desk chair. "Yes. Unfortunately, all of the major US cities were completely decimated. Those who were able to escape the cities, such as yourselves, tend to survive in rural areas in small pockets. The infection became a worldwide epidemic and the fate of international cities is apparently the same as ours."

It was a sobering thought that worldwide civilization had so quickly and easily been wiped out.

"Also unfortunately, the population of Infecteds has run out of food supplies in the cities and has been migrating into rural areas. They invaded suburban areas first, and then to slightly more remote areas. But they were unable to survive without nourishment, and weren't, for the most part, able to reach areas such as this one. They do lack the capacity to reason, which precipitated the demise of many of the Infecteds."

Arthur continued, "The remaining US military, which is mostly unharmed, does have plans to eliminate Infecteds. The most important thing I have to share with you is *not to visit any urban areas.* It will be dangerous, or deadly, to you."

"Hey, we have absolutely no desire to visit a zombie infested city," said Charlie, holding up his hands in protest.

"Not even for scavenging activities," said Arthur severely.

"No need to do that," I said. "We are following a sustainability program here. We provide for ourselves."

"What exactly is the strategy in terms of dealing with the overrun cities?" asked Charlie curiously.

The census taker pursed his lips again. "I'm not at liberty to discuss those plans."

"It's not like we're going to share them with

zombies," said Charlie in exasperation. "Even if they were able to listen to and make a plan."

Arthur hesitated. "All right. It involves the use of land mines in either a perimeter approach or on a main route in and out of a city."

Charlie nodded. "Land mines are terrible weapons. They should be banned for good by all nations. *After* we finish off the zombies."

Arthur nodded. "Testing has shown that the Infecteds don't use enough reason to stop moving forward, even when waves of Infecteds are being annihilated in front of them. But the military first had to adapt the land mines to be more explosive, so they put out fragments at about five or six feet in height to kill zombies instead of merely maim them. Although maiming certainly assisted in slowing them down."

"It must be extremely dangerous for the military to set up these land mines, though," Ty said. "Are there people spotting them?"

Arthur said, "I'm pleased to report that the military has developed bite-proof armor. It's unwieldy and wouldn't be suitable or comfortable for daily wear, but it's absolutely essential when working out in the field. I even have a suit in my sedan in case it becomes necessary."

Ty asked, "What are they like?"

"There are different kinds, but they all appear equally effective. There is a type of chainmail, for one."

Charlie gave a short laugh. "You mean like the kind that knights would wear? I guess there's no biting through *that*."

"Precisely. And the regular military armor, made of Kevlar and ceramic, doesn't do badly, either. There are more types of armor being developed."

I suddenly felt like flying a US flag out the front of the cabin. It's amazing how a capable military can make you feel very patriotic.

"What about the rural areas?" asked Ty.

"That's taking a bit longer, since the Infecteds are more scattered there. Some of them have been dispatched by armed citizens protecting their homes," said Arthur.

Charlie and I exchanged looks. I felt a pang again, thinking of Annie.

"And some are being dispatched by soldiers with machine guns. They've found it's easy to disable Infecteds by focusing on their legs and then permanently eliminating them by firing on them from there." Arthur gave a sideways glance at Ginny, clearly tempering his speech to make it less gruesome for a younger audience.

"So basically, I'm hearing that we should just stay tight. Wait for the military to do its job. Keep doing what we're doing. And now that the government knows we're here, we'll get updated later on?" asked Charlie.

"That's correct. Although I am asked to inform you that there are quite a few government-run facilities that are operating as safe camps. You're welcome to join one. I'll provide you with a map showing the locations nearest you. Generally, they're being run from rural prisons and schools," said Arthur, pulling out a few maps from his briefcase.

We passed them around. I gave Charlie a hesitant look. I knew one thing—I wanted to stay here. Why risk a possibly treacherous trip to live in the confines of a prison or school?

I was relieved when Charlie glanced around at all of our faces and said, "Thanks, Arthur. But I have the feeling that we're probably going to stay put. Please keep us updated, though."

As the census taker left, and we continued cleaning the kitchen a little more quietly than before his visit, Ginny said, "I'm so happy we're staying."

Ty applauded her statement and I gave her a hug as Charlie grinned at her. I couldn't imagine a safer refuge, surrounded by all the people that I loved.

**

Liz also writes mysteries as Elizabeth Craig.Please sign up for Elizabeth's free, no-spam newsletter for a free ebook: http://eepurl.com/kCy5j .

About the Author:

Liz (Elizabeth S. Craig) writes the Southern Quilting mysteries and Memphis Barbeque mysteries (as Riley Adams) for Penguin Random House and the Myrtle Clover series for Midnight Ink and independently. She blogs at: ElizabethSpannCraig.com/blog.

Named by Writer's Digest as one of the 101 Best Websites for Writers. Elizabeth makes her home in Matthews, North Carolina, with her husband and two teenage children.

Acknowledgments:

This was a fun and different project for me to take on. I couldn't have done it without the loving support and encouragement of my family. Thanks to Coleman, Riley, and Elizabeth Ruth. In addition, I appreciated the skillful editing from the marvelous Judy Beatty. Thanks once again to Rik Hall for formatting the book for digital and print publication. And thanks to Andrei Bat for his cover design.

Other Works by the Author:

Myrtle Clover Series in Order:

Pretty is as Pretty Dies
Progressive Dinner Deadly
A Dyeing Shame
A Body in the Backyard
Death at a Drop-In
A Body at Book Club
Death Pays a Visit
A Body at Bunco
Myrtle Clover Mysteries Sampler Volume 1
Myrtle Clover Mysteries Sampler Volume 2

Southern Quilting Mysteries in Order:

Quilt or Innocence
Knot What it Seams
Quilt Trip
Shear Trouble
Tying the Knot

Memphis Barbeque Mysteries in Order (Written as Riley Adams):

Delicious and Suspicious
Finger Lickin' Dead
Hickory Smoked Homicide
Rubbed Out

Where to Connect With Liz Craig (Elizabeth S. Craig):

Facebook: Elizabeth Spann Craig Author
Riley Adams, Author
Twitter: @elizabethscraig
Website: www.elizabethspanncraig.com

Thanks so much for reading my book...I appreciate it. If you enjoyed the story, would you please leave a short review on the site where you purchased it? Just a few words would be great. Not only do I feel encouraged reading them, but they also help other readers discover my books. Thank you!